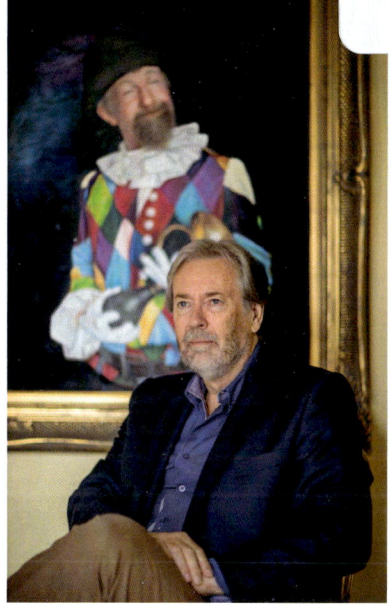

(photograph by Dylan Vaughan)

Born in Yorkshire into a family that originated from Ireland, John A. Blakey's early career was in education. He lectured in English and communications at Harrogate College of Arts and Technology, but always with an ambition to eventually become a full-time artist.

In 1990, that dream was realised, and his studio in the beautiful Yorkshire Dales was opened by fellow Yorkshireman Sir Michael Parkinson, who had invited him to stay at his home when he painted his portrait. John has painted many famous subjects, including film stars, army generals, politicians, royals and captains of industry from many countries.

His work has taken him all over the world, from Siberia where he designed costumes for performers from the State Opera, to Mombasa and Costa Rica for private commissions, and his interest in writing grew from wishing to record and share his many adventures and experiences throughout his artistic career.

John now lives in Co. Cavan in Ireland as a working artist, writer and musician.

'John Blakey is one of the leading watercolour artists of his generation who is known for his impressive style of painting portraits and still loves using traditional techniques drawn from the great masters. Watercolour is a medium that demands great skill. Painting using this medium with utmost perfection is a challenge for the most experienced artist. Using a carefully limited palette, he creates realistic portraits in a nuanced observational style that is sympathetic to his subjects without romanticizing them.

These paintings just enthrall the viewer, coming alive by capturing his subjects down to the finest detail, showing the beauty and celebrating the humanity that underlies their often rugged and weatherworn features.

John is a member of The Watercolour Society of Ireland and in 2018 was awarded the President's prize and Dr Pat McCabe Cup for his painting: "The Flower Seller of Muinchille".'

Liam O'Herlihy,
President Watercolour Society of Ireland

To my dear friend Hugo Speer.

John A. Blakey

THE LEGEND OF ICARUS O'TOOLE

The Incredible Naked Flying Man of Achill

AUSTIN MACAULEY PUBLISHERS™

LONDON • CAMBRIDGE • NEW YORK • SHARJAH

A CIP catalogue record for this title is available from the British Library.

ISBN 9781528902151 (Paperback)
ISBN 9781528906616 (Hardback)
ISBN 9781528914437 (ePub e-book)

www.austinmacauley.com

First Published (2020)
Austin Macauley Publishers Ltd
25 Canada Square
Canary Wharf
London
E14 5LQ

A Special Thanks to

Des Cafferkey, Peter Carney and Matt Molloy, who persuaded me to situate Icarus in the beautiful Achill Island in West Mayo.

Tam Gallagher for his Glaswegian tuition.

Christopher Rawcliffe for correcting my schoolboy French.

Maria Fitzpatrick for her unquestioning support.

LIST OF CHAPTERS

The Wild Sparrow

I soar just like an eagle,
yet I waddle like a duck,
With feathers like a peacock,
all clarted up with muck.
I dart as though a dragonfly,
across the crystal pond,
I'm a graceful summer swallow,
with a phony magic wand.
I'm as skittish as a creepy bug,
that crawls beneath the bed,
Where people put their boots on,
and squash me 'til I'm dead.
I've the freedom of a tumbleweed,
I'm a felon on the run.
Yet I dazzle like a hummingbird,
out flitting in the sun.
I'm as happy as a butterfly,
for this you have my word,
I'm a chirpy little sparrow,
a fly upon a turd.

Icarus' childhood home on Achill Island

THE EARLY YEARS

ICARUS O'TOOLE WAS NOT the kind of man you would meet every day. To say that he was different would be the classic understatement. He wasn't different like a zebra is to a horse, more like a bunch of rhubarb offered to a bridesmaid for her posy. He was a square peg in a round hole; a happily lost wanderer; a nature lover searching for wild orchids on a rubbish dump while grubbing in the dirt for discarded odds and sods with equal fascination.

He was an enigma: a contradictory and conflicted soul, like a smoked kipper is to the secret formula of a fine French perfume. He was a sensitive soul, while at the same time crass and vulgar. He was well read and schooled in the arts, but also beguiled by the baser things in life. He loved listening to the melodious offerings of Mozart while trying to piss over his neighbour's challengingly high fence. He was once found by his mother about to eat a wriggling handful of earthworms; he explained to her that he wanted to sing like the song thrush he'd been listening to and watching.

He was courageous and honest to a fault, kind and well meaning, but equally socially clumsy. He never lied, even if it cost him dearly. There were some who found him strange, even weird, and it must be said, considered him to be dangerous even perverted. Others believed that he should simply be locked up, but he also had many secret admirers, who wished they had the same courage to be as free spirited.

He was often surprising; not like an unexpected birthday present, but more like an unexpected fart that bursts out alarmingly whilst shaking hands with the girlfriend's mother on meeting her for the very first time. Worse than that, in Icarus's case, it would be a thunderous fart that would vibrate all the way up to her armpit, and minutes later would consecrate the room with such a stench, that it would reinforce all of her suspicions about him.

Icarus O'Toole was beautifully strange, blissfully living the life of a stargazer; eyes aloft on the nobler things of life, without watching where he was treading. He was naively unaware that at any moment he could trip and fall headlong into a very unpleasant ditch, and nose-dive he did into many such ditches. He didn't seem to mind.

He had not an ounce of badness in him – not really, but few saw it that way. He would do anything for a laugh: he used to mix ingredients up in his mammy's kitchen like many small children delight in doing, but soap powder pancakes and drain cleaner flack-jacks as he described them, were potentially lethal. His mammy nearly had a heart attack one afternoon, stopping him just in time from selling them from the little stall he had set up by the back gate. He received a good telling off, but it would have been much worse if she had found his box of cow pat and treacle pasties, and his bottles of wee-wee and dandelion beer, that he had made fizzy by stirring in a dirty great dose of Epsom salts.

Their picturesque little cottage would have become a warzone, had she found out that he had sold four bottles of the dandelion beer to Mrs McPugh, who had given them to her lethargic husband, who in turn came back the next day eagerly looking for more. Icarus' mother wondered what Mr McPugh wanted, when he stood at the door shouting enthusiastically about lead in his pencil, when without warning he belched out a bloated belly full of trapped wind that should have been given a status red weather warning. He began to gurgle and foam at the mouth as he bent double clinging on to the door for dear life. His contorted face drained to a sickly shade of green and he staggered off down the path clutching his baggy pants fore and aft, desperately straining to contain a maelstrom of evil smelling gas and bowel-bilge. He failed miserably.

"What the feck did he want?" she wondered as she went indoors to fetch a bucket of water to sluice down the path. "The dirty feckin' bastard."

From the confusion and mayhem of his misdemeanours, Icarus always beamed an innocent "who me?" smile. It was as if he had inherited the previous occupants ineffective flushing of the loo, and after several failed attempts himself, he was immediately followed in, yet again by the girlfriend's tutting mother.

He was misunderstood, condemned, castigated, humiliated and abused throughout most of his adult life, yet amazingly he never bore a grudge or whinged about anything. His adventures, or misadventures to be more accurate, were always a joy to him and he looked forward to each new day. He was a quixotic figure constantly seeking to escape by flying high above the dull greyness and callousness of everyday life.

Icarus O'Toole, or Timmy as he was christened, was born in the shadow of the mighty Croaghaun Mountain on the west of Achill Island to a single mother, Mary O'Toole. His childhood was impoverished, but only by lack of money. For a young boy to be raised in such a magnificent and truly beautiful part of the world was wonderful. Icarus was able to run wild and free as the gales that blew across the Atlantic towards their tiny rose covered cottage by the sea at Keem strand. It moulded his character and nurtured a spirit in him that would never leave him, even in his most troubling days.

— *Icarus' Mammy* —

His mammy adored him, and they had a very special bond, perhaps more so because his wayward father had disappeared like a feather in the breeze when he was just a few days old. From that day on, she flatly refused to speak of him.

As a toddler he loved chasing about naked along the towering cliffs of Croaghaun, and the neighbouring Minaun cliffs, the highest in the whole of Europe. He loved to feel the rushing breeze caress his skin and tousle his hair, as he wildly chased about screaming like a hungry seagull. Even in the depths of winter he raced about the cliff tops, with his mother chasing breathlessly behind with a warm blanket and a flask of hot tea. He giggled uncontrollably yelling, "Wicked!" and described in detail how the fresh air blew around his willy and made it wobble and 'flop-a-lop' about. All well and good when he was an innocent boy of three, but he was bound to be in trouble as he grew into adulthood. Of course, he never did grow up, not in his heart, he never wanted to, but in reality, he eventually grew to be a towering six-feet ten inches tall. In time his cries of "wicked" would come to have a more literal meaning for some, and would be used callously against him by those who wished to do him harm.

It was some years however, before Timmy would face any of the difficulties that would challenge his later life, and even though his mammy had a struggle to get him to put on his clothes in order to go to school, he was a keen pupil and had a very happy time there. He loved to learn; he didn't just read books, he attacked them with a ravenous enthusiasm, always hungry for more. He was curious about everything, his favourite word being "why?" He drove his teachers and all around him mad with it: "Why is the sky blue and not red?" he would demand to know. "And why is water so wet? Why don't ducks sink? Why is food so tasty but Brussels sprouts taste like shite? Why did my daddy leave me?"

He was very popular among his classmates for he was very kind and helpful to all – teachers included. Timmy was as bright as a button and retained knowledge like a sponge, in fact he was outstanding at everything that he tried, but he never showed off, or tried to take advantage of his rapidly accumulating skills and learning. He also was eager to assist his fellow pupils with arithmetic and spelling or any other subject if they found it a struggle, and always in a caring way so as not to make them look silly or stupid: "You knew the answer all along," he would say, "it just got stuck and wouldn't come out."

It was only the caretaker Mr Sneer, who didn't like Timmy; he liked to mock him shouting out: "The only job you'll get when you leave here O'Toole, is a road-sweeper, cos you're as daft as a brush." Mind you, it was usually a response to something Timmy had done, such as the time he dyed his hair bright yellow because he wanted to be like a daffodil and 'wander lonely as a cloud', like Willy Wordsworth. His daft behaviour wasn't such a problem then, or so obvious; it was much later when it started to stick out like a baboon's bare bum.

—————— Wandering lonely as a cloud ——————

Timmy O'Toole was given the nickname Icarus by a sweet girl in his class called Daisy Maisie. She was called so, because she spent much of the long summer days making delicate daisy-chains and hanging them tenderly about people's necks, claiming them as her own very special friend. She thought Timmy was wonderful and liked to hold his hand as he gazed longingly into the blue yonder, admiring the graceful circling seagulls and their freedom. Of course, Timmy adored her right back; he loved her delicate ways, her pretty face and her winning smile. She was the warm summer breeze and the scents of the wild flower meadows all in one.

"Someday you'll fly Timmy, I just know it, just like Icarus from Greek legend; up there with the dickybirds. From now I'll call you Icarus... Icarus O'Toole," and she smiled at him in admiration. Timmy had read about the story of Icarus and how he flew too close to the sun, melting the wax that held in his feathers, and how he crashed into the sea, but he supposed that Superglue was not available then in the shops of ancient Greece. He also didn't see any significance in relation to himself, that the story of Icarus ended in tragedy.

"What an incredible idea," he thought to himself, "I'll become Icarus O'Toole. I'll design and build a personal flying kit and launch myself into the heavens." He was ever so proud of his new nickname and proclaimed: "The flying will be spectacular, I'll be able to see from above the verdant forests and snow-capped mountains and crystal-clear rivers in all of their beauty. I'll be able to glide in and out of candyfloss clouds and fly through colour drenched rainbows. I'll rise up and be engulfed by magnificent sunsets and find peace and solitude flitting among the twinkly night stars; but better still, like a seagull I'll be able to plop on the heads of unsuspecting people down below!"

One day, Sergeant Fitzdick came to speak to his mother about her mischievous son: "Now look here Mrs O'Toole, we're having a few complaints. Your Timmy has been up to his usual tricks again."

"It's Ms O'Toole to you," she insisted, "Not married, never will be. Do you think I'd be a fetcher and carrier to some dirty unshaven drunk that likes to reward you with the back of his hand... well do you?"

"Mary, if I may call you that..."

"No, you may not you bollix!" she snapped back. "And can't you leave my Timmy alone? He's no harm at all, he's just a wild little sparrow."

"Not so little now Ms O'Toole. He'll be fifteen next, and he's already well over six feet tall. Anyway, he's been storming the cliffs, stark bollock naked and acting the maggot as usual, but this time he's made a big mistake. He's crashed headlong into Miss Penelope, Squire Hobnob's daughter while she was taking her morning stroll. She's been away to Queen Sillyburgher's Finishing School for Superior Girls in England and has only just arrived home. What you describe as a wild little sparrow, has become a rather large cock. Poor Penelope might never recover from the shock: your Timmy's given her a finishing school all of his own."

"I must inform you officially, that this is to be Timmy's last warning. I'll try and smooth things over with the Squire, but I can't keep making excuses for him. It's only a matter of time before he faces the full force of the law. He can't go on like this, why only five minutes ago, I had a phone-call from some elderly English tourists, bleating about some out of control hooligan, high on the cliffs, naked as the day he was born, stuffing a goose feather up his arse while singing 'It's a long way to Tipperary' – I wonder who that could be now?"

"I'll have a word with him," she replied with a sigh, "but he's a wild little sparrow, he won't be caged."

— Sergeant Fitzdick —

19

Sergeant Fitzdick nodded resignedly and closed the rickety cottage door behind him gently. Minutes later it bust open dramatically and young Timmy planted himself in the door frame like an opera singer who had been given his first major role at Covent Garden, and all of the critics were in the front row.

"Taaaaarraaaaa!" he exclaimed with an extravagant gesture of his right hand and a flick of a goose feather in his left, but his enthusiastic entrance wilted when he could see that his mother was quiet and troubled.

"We can't go on like this, Timmy. I've had Sergeant Fitzdick here again. Something about you scaring Penelope Hobnob half to death."

"It was an accident mammy, I was chasing this goose around for one of its feathers, for my flying costume you see, when she came out of nowhere..."

"I'm sure it was son, but aren't you ever cold on those windy cliff tops without a stitch on? I'm sure you'll end up with pneumonia, and it'll be me who has to look after you and pay for a doctor and buy the medicine which we can't afford. We have so little money Timmy, I needed a pair of shoes last winter, and I'm still wearing this worn out pair... oh, Timmy I'm at the end of my tether, I wish I had someone to look after me!"

She began to cry and tried to hide her tears from him. "Don't worry mammy, I'll look after you. I can get a Saturday job on Alice Slapcabbage's farm. I know they're looking for manual workers to load hay and things into their barn lofts, and I can reach out of reach stuff really easily."

"Alice Slapcabbage won't give you a job son, she thinks you're bonkers, and her uncle, who actually owns the farm thinks you're certifiable, he says it's you who should be put out of reach!"

"Just because I..."

"That's enough Timmy," interrupted his mammy sharply. "We won't go into that again."

Timmy cuddled up to his mammy as she stared blankly out of the broken kitchen window that she could not afford to have mended. Her fears for her son and the future were deeply troubling to her. She had an impending sense of helplessness and disaster. She looked up at her wayward son, who was flapping his arms Icarus fashion, while examining his precious goose feather. She stood up and gently teased the goose feather from his hand to catch his full attention and was just about to suck on it like a fountain pen when he managed to snatch it back just in time. She looked at him puzzled and then kissed him and hugged him with a loving and tenderness that only Irish mammies know how. She accepted fully that he was away with the fairies and that's where he was happiest, and that's how he wanted to be.

For the rest of the summer and well into the autumn, Timmy went to school, came home and whizzed straight up onto the cliffs and stayed there until almost dark. Throughout Achill and even on the mainland, a tale of a boc* goat that lived on the cliffs of Croaghaun had been growing into legend. A fearsome monster of a goat had been seen disappearing into the low clouds and mist, and the locals were becoming so scared that they would not allow their children anywhere near the summit. As the myth grew, so did the size of the goat. Very soon it had lethal horns like huge bayonets, and its long grey beard and cloven hooves established it as a reincarnated evil spirit or even Satan himself.

Deep into the winter and during the dark hours it was reported that Icarus

The Devil Rider

*   Gaelic: buck; a playboy

21

could be seen racing naked along the silhouette of the clifftops with the horned beast by his side. Rumours were growing that Timmy was in league with the devil, and that he indulged in naked sacrilegious ceremonies in the dead of night when the moon was full.

The truth of it was that the boc goat came to trust Icarus as he got used to his presence on the mountain and his untamed ways. They were kindred spirits and became great buddies, and they would often descend Croaghaun together where Icarus fed him in his back garden with scraps that his mammy had saved. For those that the boc goat trusted, it was a very gentle creature, but it was a fearsome sight for the nervous or belligerent of nature. It also was very territorial, and part of its domain became the O'Toole's cottage and garden, which made Timmy's mammy feel protected and secure, especially as she was on her own so much of the time.

"Be careful Timmy," implored his mammy, "there are whispers on the island about you and the goat. I know that there are many who are damning of me, because I had you out of wedlock, but they seem to have it in for you even more. People see what they want to see, and if they can condemn you, they will, especially if they see an opportunity."

"But he's only a goat," he protested, "he's as gentle as a lamb with me, and he even butts me away from the cliff edge if he feels I am getting too close, and anyway most folk think he doesn't exist at all."

The next day after school, Timmy as usual headed up the path to the top of Croaghaun. It was already growing dark as he carried a sack full of turnip tops for his friend. Descending towards him was a pack of angry looking men carrying candles and shillelaghs, followed by the parish priest with an open Bible. One of the men bumped Icarus out of the way with a glare and said: "At least that's one devil got rid of!"

Timmy raced up to the cliffs to look for his pet goat and he was passed by two grumbling men as they emerged from the low cloud. He overheard one complaining to the other that the whole idea of a devil goat was a load of bollix. He remarked that the

The Boc Goat

goat was just a wild creature of the mountains and that it should have been left to wander free. The other man observed that the exorcism couldn't have worked anyway as the wind on the top of Croaghaun kept blowing out the candles which rendered the service invalid.

"It doesn't work unless the light of Heaven can see into the darkness of Hell; you know, the angels need clear view to be able to cast the demon out!"

"Superstitious shite!" he insisted. "That holy Joe of a priest has everyone in hysterics with his tales of eternal damnation and the fires of Hell. He really believes he has rescued us, by exorcising an evil beast that was waiting to prey on the innocents of our community. I heard him tell old Tommy Flynn that he saw it throw itself off the cliffs, just like that herd of swine in the Bible. Well in the dark and mist, I saw the crafty old goat slip away towards the deserted village by Slievemore. I'm glad he's free – he is a magnificent animal; so hold your tongue Pat and leave it be."

Icarus felt sad when he overheard that his pet goat was gone, but was resigned to its fate and relieved that it was free. From time to time he heard a rumour that the boc goat had been spotted on the Minaun cliffs, after some drunken eejit* had braved the cliffs to prove his manhood. However, it was never captured and eventually all talk of it faded away into folklore.

Daisy Maisie had seen it several times before with Icarus, and even made a daisy chain for it, which it nibbled hungrily straight away and then demanded another. She then lovingly and artistically decorated his horns with daisies, which he frustratingly could not reach. After being teased to distraction he then went nuts, bucking and rearing to get at the delicious flowers – apparently, daisies are like caviar to boc goats. A hiker on the mountain that day witnessed the goings on and bravely ran to her aid, but did a sharp about-turn as the angry goat rampaged after him and chased him the whole way down to the sea. Even when he was up to his waist in the breaking waves the goat did not stop.

---

* Irish slang: an intellectually challenged fuckwit.

The well-intended but misguided hero spluttered and splashed halfway to Clare Island, before he realised that he was safe.

The following spring had been a special time for both Icarus and Daisy Maisie. The weather had been beautiful and they had spent every hour they possibly could together. It was for that reason that just before the Easter school holidays, Icarus (as he now insisted he be called) was full of concern that Daisy Maisie had not been at her school desk all week. He missed her, and was anxious to share his adventurous plans with her for the holidays. He also wanted to know if she had heard about the unidentified creature that was nibbling underwear on the washing lines of the cottages by the Minaun cliffs. He was disappointed that he had not spoken to her, but he was expecting to see her at Alice Slap-cabbage's farm, where he had managed to secure a Saturday job.

Daisy Maisie was Alice's young cousin, and worked part-time on the farm herself. She had somehow persuaded Alice to give Icarus a job, to which she reluctantly agreed, so long as he wasn't

Daisy Maisie

allowed near the slurry tank especially on April fool's day as happened last year. Daisy Maisie did basic secretarial duties, answered the phone, made pots of tea and most importantly to the Slapcabbages, kept an eye on Icarus's unpredictable and eccentric behaviour. It seemed to work out to everyone's satisfaction and they had every opportunity to enjoy each other's company. Icarus was a good honest and hard-working addition to the farm, grateful to earn a little pocket money to help ease the burden on his poor mammy. That Saturday however, when he turned up for work, all was strangely quiet.

There was none of the usual vehicles in the yard apart from Alice's uncle's beat-up old transit van with the back doors wide open. He walked over to the farmhouse kitchen, where Daisy Maisie used to welcome him with a hot cup of tea and a smile, but she was nowhere to be found. He called out her name, but she made no reply. He thought he heard something from the large barn, where they would often share their sandwiches and he went to investigate. The barn was filled with bales of hay and the air was full of dust. It was flooded with sunlight from the high roof windows and Icarus squinted to see. He could see a shape move by the back stall and he stepped towards it and called Daisy Maisie's name tenderly.

The next thing he knew was a terrible thump on the back of his shoulders and he was sent flying. His head was spinning and he was aware that he was being kicked viciously all over as someone was brutally tying chains around his ankles.

"Hoist him up, the dirty feckin' bastard. The filthy pervert is going to get his arse kicked right between the eyes."

The next voice that spoke, Icarus could only just recognise as Daisy Maisie's uncle's through his ringing ears. "We're going to teach you a lesson now you slimy gobshite; something that your useless father should have taught you years ago."

Icarus was hoisted upside down using a block and tackle, and he took a barbaric blow from a chain-clad fist right between the legs. He convulsed in agony and was so terrified that he began to choke on his own vomit. Three more men whom Icarus could not see clearly, began beating him viciously with hurling sticks.

Through his blurred vision, he could have sworn he saw the dog collar of his own parish priest, but he could not be certain.

"Now we know why you wanted to work here, you disgusting pile of dog shit. You thought you could get away with interfering with Daisy Maisie without being noticed, did you? I suspected it myself; you spent just a little too much time together in the barn. Anyway (Icarus took another huge punch between his legs) deny it if you dare, Mr Sneer overheard you at school in the corner of the playground, laughing with her about it. Anyway, she's been sent packing, the dirty little hoor* and you'll never see her again – not never, no how!"

Icarus had not the foggiest what they were talking about, and he took such a severe beating that day that he was bed-ridden for almost a year. He had five broken ribs a collapsed lung, a damaged spleen that had to be removed, and life-threatening blood clots on his brain. His jaw was shattered in four places and his face and body were so swollen and bruised, that the true extent of his injuries could not be seen.

Everyone knew who had beaten him so callously, but no one would, or dare speak up. There were those who were delighted at his fate; some were genuinely shocked, but not a Christian soul came forward to offer even the tiniest help or sympathy. When he was dumped onto his mammy's doorstep, she was absolutely distraught and implored Sergeant Fitzdick to help them.

"Oh, I heard about the accident," he tutted dismissively. "Maybe now he'll learn not to get too close to the edge of the cliffs he spends so much time gadding about on. He was very lucky you know, that the Slapcabbages just happened to be passing by."

For most of his recovery, the swelling meant that Icarus's eyes were jammed tight shut. Doctor Mead was not sure if his sight had been affected, but he had no sympathy as Mary O'Toole still had his outstanding medical bill that she had not paid. He seemed to enjoy telling her that her son's injuries meant that he would never be able to have children of his own. She was heartbroken for her son and heartbroken for herself. For weeks Icarus would

---

*   Irish slang: an affectionate woman in need of hard cash.

drift in and out of consciousness but she refused to leave his side. She prayed that he was safe in the comfort of his dreams, and able to remember his lovely Daisy Maisie and their wild chases over the cliffs of Croaghaun.

Icarus's mother guessed that those locals who were 'holier than thou' had rid themselves of Daisy Maisie. She heard that she had been dragged to the doctors after complaining of feeling sick in the mornings. Her unsympathetic mother had also noticed a little swelling about her middle. Doctor Mead made the correct diagnosis and after an emergency family meeting involving the parish priest and Gardaí, she was callously sent away to an institution to seek redemption and to make her pay for her wickedness. In the space of just two hours, she was packed up and despatched to St Vergüenza's home for wayward girls, to cleanse her soul together with the dirty laundry of the well to do.

Poor Daisy Maisie hadn't a clue; not a sinner explained to her that she was with child, least of all how it could have happened, but she was banished to a life of drudgery and hell, by those who should have been protecting her. Those same smug and sanctimonious people had their culprit and their justification; and with the Church on their side, they felt they had done God and their community proud.

Daisy Maisie had a truly petrifying time when she first arrived on the mainland to St Vergüenza's. Her hair was roughly cropped short using blunt sheep shears by a nasty little baldy man from the local village, who really enjoyed doing what he considered to be his holy duty. Then she was stripped naked and mocked, washed and deloused in front of all of the other girls and nuns. The local man who had pretended to leave, had slipped behind the door-curtain unnoticed apart from Daisy Maisie. Beyond all endurance, she met his lecherous stare with her own imploring eyes, recoiled at his drooling tobacco-stained grin as the curtain jerked up and down about his middle.

She was left totally alone lying naked on the cold stone floor for ages. Eventually, a coarse grey tunic was brought in by another girl who tossed it on the floor and gestured for her to put it on. She then beckoned her to follow her to the laundry-room where she explained her duties to her, what the prayer and meal times were, and how it would be a good idea for the selfish bitch to show a little gratitude to those who were most generously giving her food and shelter.

One day, while she was scrubbing hard with red-raw hands at some disgustingly stained bed sheets, a pious nun began to pick at her and goad her. She called her 'Daisy the dirty Maisie' as she mockingly rubbed her own fat belly and pointed at Daisy's. Daisy Maisie finally snapped and flew at her, biting her hard on the arm. She let out such a shriek, that the rest of the nuns came flying in like a flock of carrion crows. The Mother Superior, Sister Rencoroso, slapped the hysterical nun and then turned her wrath towards Daisy Maisie. She stooped over her victim with her beaky nose pressing hard against her pale cheek; her vile breath made her recoil in disgust. The Mother Superior loved feeling powerful; she believed absolutely that her brutality was a kindness to the girls in the long term. Sister Rencoroso suffered from halitosis of the soul.

"So, you are a biter then as well as slapper, you... you vicious unholy wastrel. Your perfect teeth and pretty smile are the temptress' tools of Satan – well we will have to fix that for you. Your Jezebel smile put you in here, but in order for you to find salvation, we must wipe that smile completely from your face. We have to rescue you from yourself; it will be our holy gift to you."

Daisy Maisie was forced into and locked up in a tiny cold cell and waited in the dark for what seemed like hours. Then with a heavy metallic crash the door burst open and hovering above her like a dark hawk was the Mother Superior with her tooled-up handyman in a grubby white coat. With the assistance of two other nuns, she was ferociously strapped down into the wooden chair in the corner of the room. Horrific heart-breaking cries shattered the silence of the stark corridors, as the unqualified dentist and part-time hairdresser ripped every single tooth from her pretty little mouth.

Daisy Maisie was left alone all night without even a glass of water, to think about her degenerate ways and to pray for forgiveness. In the morning, the Mother Superior with a gloating smile, brought in a mirror for her to see for herself how she had been brought down to earth. Daisy wept; her body and soul had been desecrated. Her smile that she loved to share with Icarus had been most cruelly stolen, and her red swollen eyes and bloody torn gums made her look grotesque. She was broken into a thousand pieces.

A week later, almost in a hypnotic state, Daisy Maisie accidently fell through the laundry drying-room door which had not been bolted properly from the outside. She had been leaning against it, dreaming of sunny days with Icarus, when she found herself in the open yard used for hanging wet sheets. Unnoticed she wandered in a daze to the back gate which had been left unlocked in anticipation of a delivery of washing soda. She pushed open the gate and set off like an earthbound wraith in no particular direction until she was absolutely exhausted. She was not missed for hours as the nuns were used to her 'sulking' and spending long periods on her own.

Daisy Maisie could only think of one thing, and that was to return to the place where she had known great happiness. The fresh sea breezes over the high cliffs of Croaghaun called to her, and she longed for the gentleness and warmth of her Icarus. Wearily she tramped for hours on end, sleeping hidden in shucks* by day and walking by night so not to be caught.

After countless days, starving and weak, she found herself high on her beloved cliffs. With a trembling voice she desperately called out for Icarus, but her feeble cries faded unanswered over the dark ocean beyond the cliffs. An old man walking his dog stopped to see if she was in need of any assistance. He smiled at her with concern but recoiled when he saw her mutilated face. He was horrified, but he guessed who she was, and with sympathy, informed her that Timmy O'Toole was long gone, never ever to return. He believed he was doing her a favour.

A full harvest moon had just risen, and the delicious evening air and landscape all about her were breathtakingly beautiful.

---

* Irish slang: ditch, usually filled with water.

Sister Rencoroso and St Vergüenza's

She closed her pretty eyes, and with a piteous sigh said, "He could never love me, not looking like this," and she simply stepped over the edge of the cliffs. Her body was never found. She was not quite sixteen, still a child and completely unaware that she carried a small child inside her. Not a single soul searched for her. She was an embarrassing problem conveniently forgotten and swept under a very dirty carpet.

One man who knew of Daisy Maisie's fate wrote an anonymous letter to Mrs O'Toole, but she feared to tell Icarus of her tragic end. She knew that his broken body would not be helped to heal by a broken heart, for he might never recover.

She was right of course, but the decision to tell him or not was taken out of her hands. She died of pneumonia later that winter, cold and half-starved with a pile of unpaid medical bills. Icarus's recuperation was not helped by a doctor who was more concerned about his remuneration than his patient's welfare. He eventually abandoned him to 'let nature take its course', as he dismissively put it.

Despite everything, Icarus did begin to mend, but he was not to be the same. His memory had been affected and he displayed a strangeness in his character that was stained with a profound sadness. Many things that had been part of his life were lost or confused at best.

He could not remember the name of the sweet girl who had been a lovely figment of his fantasy dream world that he had wandered in and out of for almost a year. He had no recollection of his mother at all, and he was confused when a small bundle of her belongings was thrown outside of his bedroom door, together with a pile of medical bills and a solicitor's demand for prompt payment.

When he gathered a little strength and was able to walk a few steps, he took little turns about his cottage and later along the sands. Once a week, on his return, he would find a box of food and other goodies waiting for him on the doorstep. He had a Good Samaritan caring for him, but whoever it was, was very secretive and he never caught them making their clandestine delivery. This kindness kept him going as he had absolutely no money to pay for such basic necessities, and day by day he grew a little stronger.

A month later still lost and fuzzy, he returned from his little stroll by the sea. He was alarmed to see that his belongings, furniture and all, were being tossed out of his bedroom window and dragged out of his back door. A large wooden plank had been nailed across his front door with an attached official stamped certificate. It read: **'STRICTLY NO ENTRY, by order of the court. Property of Doctor Mead.'**

Icarus did not bother to pick up any of his belongings, he just turned his back and shrugged and set off as fast as his long but still painful legs would allow. "Well that's that," he sighed resignedly, and headed out up to his magnificent cliffs. He stood there for hours, perplexed and struggling to remember how things had been for him before. He stretched himself up to his full height, and half in a daze, he ripped all of his clothes off and braced himself against the gale that had suddenly blown up. He leant forward recklessly into the teeth of the gale which supported him like the wind in a sail, and he inched further forward out over the cliffs, tempting, even demanding fate to draw him to his death. "A lost soul with nothing, has feck-all to lose," he cried.

Over to his left in the distance he could see a gathering. A noisy posse was heading his way with burning torches and mad dogs straining at the leash. He stood still as a statue, closed his eyes

Doctor Mead

33

and pretended to be invisible. He was quickly surrounded by a baying mob who were screaming obscenities at him and demanding for him to be taken away. Shortly afterwards the alarm bell of a secure ambulance could be heard arriving at Keem Strand some two thousand feet below, and two burly male nurses jumped out, raced up like mountain goats and wrestled him to the ground. They then knelt on him as they roughly strapped him into a cruelly tight straitjacket. Sergeant Fitzdick half-heartedly tried to protect him from a hail of blows that rained down upon him as they dragged him down the mountainside, and then helped bundle him into the back of the ambulance.

He travelled with him at high speed, bells ringing and lights flashing, to Slack-water House, the secure mental institution hidden among the peaks of Macbillygoat's Reeks in County Kerry. It was a very uncomfortable journey of some three hundred and fifty kilometres, where Icarus bounced about painfully from side to side and up and down. Apart from the straitjacket, he had been deliberately left unsecured out of sheer spite. Icarus had been unceremoniously cast out from his beautiful Achill, as far away as could be organised, with a coldness and loathing that was shameful.

Nearly six hours later on arriving at Slack-water House, Icarus was helped inside in a surprisingly gentle way by the staff who were all waiting for him with a sympathetic curiosity. Sergeant Fitzdick hastily completed the paperwork and signed the documents that committed him to ten long years of electric shock and cold-water treatment. He refused even to look at Icarus as he left, let alone say goodbye as he jumped back into the ambulance. Agitated and impatient, he urged the driver to put his foot down and get out of there as fast as he could. Like Pontius Pilate of old, he was attempting to wash his hands of an inconvenient problem, and his own guilty conscience at the same time.

For a full decade Icarus languished there. The aches and pains from his dreadful beatings never fully went away, but he learned, 'mind over matter' from Mrs Bigley, a particularly caring nurse, and ever so slowly, he began to cope. After a while they abandoned the electric shock treatment as a waste of time, but they kept on with the cold-water showers as he really enjoyed them. He used to sing on the top of his voice all kinds of nonsensical things which had his carers falling about laughing, and of course he loved being naked and wet. He never lost his sweet caring nature, nor his sense of fun, but he could not reclaim much of his past memories. Miraculously, he was still highly intelligent, but his reality and fantasy world would often merge into one, being unable at times to tell them apart.

Strangely, his memory of Icarus resurfaced, and he would tell his carers fabulous tales, such as how he liked to fly around the great pyramids of Egypt on his way to visit Cleopatra, and how he had just come back from swooping over the Eiffel Tower after calling in to the Moulin Rouge for a bowl of French onion soup. In the craft workshop, he had designed and created his flying costume, which he made from offcuts of leather and bits of brass. He made wings with straps attached for stability, and borrowed a dashing white scarf from Doctor de Grave for style. He found a pair of discarded motorcycle goggles under a bench in the staff garage and made a quiver from a piece of old canvas to contain his flight feathers. His carers showed an encouraging interest in his efforts and they all grew to be very fond of him, but they became a bit anxious when he began to stick the feathers up his arse.

Icarus had been a rare and fine porcelain vase that had been knocked carelessly from the mantelpiece. He had shattered into many pieces; some large, some tiny, some lost. With loving care, he had been painstakingly put back together again by the staff at Slack-water House. Many of the cracks would always be visible; some pieces were only an approximation of their original position, but at least he was whole once more – after a fashion. He remained unaware however, of how fragile he was and how the slightest of knocks could shatter him forever.

Slack-water House held other inmates even more fragile than he, but it was only rumour and gossip that reached the ears of the other less afflicted patients. The truth was, that high in the attics behind locked and bolted heavy oak doors, resided the saddest cases. At night piteous cries and wails called out to the moon and made everyone's blood run cold. Icarus buried his head under his pillow, fearing that he had been only a whisker away from being incarcerated up there himself.

There was tale of old Fanny who had been left in a telephone box as a new-born baby. No one came to claim her, and eventually she was placed into foster-care. Something happened there that everyone refused to speak about, and without warning, she was roughly gathered up and dispatched to Slack-water House like a sack of spuds dumped at the scullery door. All of her time locked away, she continually sobbed as she scrubbed her hands, cursing to herself that she must scour her dirty body and soul clean. She scrubbed so hard to remove the filth that her hands turned into open sores, and soap and brushes had to be confiscated from her. In her sixty-eight years at Slack-water house, not one soul ever came to visit her, neither did she ever receive a single letter, or a solitary birthday card.

Also, it was rumoured that an old farmer called Ted, had to be permanently subdued by a cocktail of drugs because he was so wild and dangerous. Apparently, he came from a remote farm, high in the hills of Connemara, where he had lived happily with his old mother. When she died suddenly, he had some kind of breakdown and after four months of not being seen, he was found by neighbours slumped in his chair staring blankly out of his kitchen window. His two faithful dogs were starving and had turned vicious, and the Gardaí had to shoot them dead as they tried to protect old Ted from being taken to hospital. Having lost his dear mother, the violent loss of his faithful dogs drove him into such a state of madness and confusion, that he was never able to find his way back to normality or any kind of peace.

One of the kitchen porters had told Icarus about another patient called Michael Mann, who had been there so long he had outstayed three complete changes of staff and administration. His history was a little sketchy, but in an old dog-eared file, he had been classified as 'broken beyond repair'. Apparently, he had so deeply loved a maiden – the fairest in all the broad land – that his passion had driven him to insanity. He at times like Icarus, could not distinguish reality from fantasy.

The story went that he had met with a sorcerous and mysterious raven, who predicted that Michael would kill his own true love. He was so incensed that he struck down the raven with a dagger made of fire and steel, and then found his true love lying on the ground mortally wounded before him. Crazy man Michael, as he came to be known, was a tragic figure who ranted and raved and waved his fists in utter despair, and reminded everyone, medical staff included, of how fragile the thread is that secures and safeguards our sanity, and keeps us from falling into the chaos of madness.

Icarus often dwelt hard on the matter: "How can one love too much? How can love turn in ourselves, and devour us like a flesh-eating worm? We are all miserable beings."

The story of Michael Mann, lodged in the back of Icarus's mind and from time to time, in the dead of night, it haunted him, and so he prayed like crazy that he would not lose his mind in such a way. He was unaware of his love for his lost Daisy, or how it been discovered and torn from him and callously smothered. It was Icarus's beautiful yet sad and forgotten dream.

During his final year with them however, his mischievous nature began to show itself once more. He got up to all kinds of tricks and practical jokes and was always forgiven with a smile. He began to read again, and all kinds of possibilities and ideas started to brew and fester. After reading Chaucer and discovering Rabelais he worked on his language skills, believing that polite hypocrisy was the enemy of truth. He had the staff and other patients in stitches as he explained: "To call someone a bollix, hits the nail on the head: feck off you bollix means so much more than please leave me alone, you have offended me!" Day by day his language became more creatively blue and the staff began to worry about Slack-water House's reputation when Icarus was finally presented to polite society once more.

"What a sloppy piss-pot of a day!" he would shout if it rained when he wanted to go out. "What a perfect picturesque pink nipple of a day!" he would sing if it was sunny.

Unfortunately, some of the other patients began to mimic him, but they lacked his sense of theatre and irony. Even Icarus was alarmed when old Mr McTweezer greeted Nurse Bigley one particularly sunny spring morning: "Grand morning," he grinned, "you hairy arsed fat ugly cunt!"

Icarus O'Toole had been a frightened and fragile young *garsún** of seventeen when he first arrived at Slack-water House. He was a towering six feet ten, when at twenty-seven it was time to leave, carrying the bold confidence reminiscent of a one-armed trapeze artist: strong and fearless but ill equipped.

He had been quite a handsome if somewhat gangly youth, but sadly after his injuries, he was strange to look at, and his newly cultivated little turned-up moustache didn't help. He had grown it to give himself a more mature appearance for when he left, but it made him look even sillier. His shock of bright red hair and his misshapen snout of a nose meant that his carers were more than a little worried about how he would be received by the world outside. In the consultant's notes of his discharge papers, Doctor de Grave wrote: 'Icarus O'Toole is no danger to himself or society in general. He is like a lighthouse in the middle of the Bog of Allen; bright but absolutely useless.'

On the day he was to leave, the whole of Slack-water House; doctors, nurses, carers, kitchen staff and all, came out to say goodbye. Nurse Bigley's four-year-old daughter ran out and threw her arms about him, and gave him a parting gift of her favourite and very precious dolly. The whole gathering clapped and cheered like lunatics as he turned to walk to the end of the drive to catch the midday bus to Dingle. He looked over his shoulder and smiled sweetly at the little girl. "What's the dolly's name?" he asked.

"Daisy," she smiled, "after the pretty flowers in the meadows."

"Would bring a tear to a glass eye," sniffled Mr McTweezer.

"So it would," replied Doctor de Grave, not noted for bouts of sentimentality. "Indeed, it does!"

* Gaelic: young fella.

Mr McTweezer and Slackwater House

POETRY IN MOTION

CARUS WAS MET AT the bus station in Dingle by Miss Eva Caber, the social worker appointed to oversee his transition from inmate at Slack-water House to inmate of the outside world as she put it. Eva was a good natured if somewhat cynical Scot, brought up in the toughest neighbourhood of Glasgow. She had a wicked sense of humour and was a force to be reckoned with: she also didn't suffer fools gladly. She was fiercely protective of those in her care and was terrifying when crossed. Icarus was in very safe hands.

"Welcome to the madhouse," she smiled as she attempted to give Icarus a welcome kiss on the cheek. Her five-feet-one-inch stature, even with heels, left her woefully short of Icarus's towering frame. "Feck me, you're as tall as a tree," she gasped as she made to pick up his small scruffy suitcase.

"It's okay," he replied, "the suitcase, not my being tall, well no – I mean yes, I like being tall, I can reach all kinds of..."

"This way!" interrupted Eva as she pushed through the crowd, batting people out of the way with his tatty suitcase, "Gangway!"

Icarus followed her through the tourist-filled streets until they came to the quayside where she told him to sit down while she went to buy them both an ice cream. "Get your laughing tackle around that," she grinned as she took a huge suck on her cornet. "Feckin' adore ice-cream... better than sex!"

Icarus had found a kindred spirit in the language arena, but he wondered to himself what on earth sex were. He didn't ask her to explain as he didn't want to appear stupid, he just agreed with a smile: "Delicious... a creamy vanilla rollercoaster of a feckin' taste fantasia!"

"I see you're quite a poet," observed Eva which opened a conversation about words and their true meanings and all kinds of deep philosophical things. Their animated discourse went on all afternoon and only ended when they gazed open mouthed in wonderment at the stunning sunset over the deep blue Atlantic that lay before them.

"Time to go," said Eva as she snatched up Icarus's suitcase and pushed his hand away. She was already very fond of him.

She took him to her little flat on the outskirts of the town and informed him that he could stay with her until he got sorted out. After showing him where he was to sleep, Icarus sat on the end of the camp bed that she had provided for him and switched off the little bedside lamp. He lay back with hands clasped behind his head and let out a contented sigh which exploded into a surprised scream. The temporary and rickety camp bed and Icarus's overlong body could not find a friendly equilibrium, and he was sent somersaulting into Eva's expensive Connemara-green velvet curtains. "What the farkle-twatters!" he shrieked, but then he snuggled the luxurious fabric about him like a cocoon, "A perfect picturesque pink nipple of a day," he murmured as he drifted off into a delicious sleep.

Eva found him in the morning as she brought him a nice hot cup of tea. He looked like a giant butterfly wriggling to escape from a giant chrysalis. "What the feck!" she cried in dismay and anger, concerned for her prized curtains which had been left to her by her favourite aunty Bridie. But then she burst into whoops of laughter at his confused and straggly head which poked out and emitted distressed little moans, as he repeatedly tumbled over and crashed into the furniture whilst attempting to stand up and free himself.

After the slapstick show was over, they sat down together to have a good laugh and breakfast together at Eva's little table by the window that overlooked the shoreline. Eva had a large file from Slack-water House about Icarus, but she wanted to know directly from him as much as he could remember. She was particularly interested in how he had become homeless, and how it was that he had signed the deeds of his little cottage in Achill, over to a Doctor Mead, during the earliest days of his time at Slack-water House. He was obviously not compos mentis at that stage, and still a minor, and certainly shouldn't have been signing anything. She concluded correctly that some jiggery-pokery had gone on. Icarus had not been aware that the little cottage had been left to him in his mother's will, and because he couldn't remember his mammy at all, he was easy meat.

"The feckin' slimy arsehole," she bellowed, and she swore that she would get his cottage back and give the twat-arsed cheating bollix a Glasgow kiss* that would require at least a dozen stitches. She told Icarus to make himself comfortable and relax for a day or so, and that there was plenty of food in the fridge. Eva Caber was on the warpath, all five feet one inches of Celtic fury with a rapier-like tongue to match.

She set off immediately on her sit-up-and-beg bicycle, basket over the front wheel, fuelled with a steely determination to catch a boat ride from a fisherman friend to Galway. Furiously, she biked to Doctor Mead's main surgery near Tuam in Galway, intending to doorstep and embarrass him into doing the right thing in restoring Icarus's home. She waited for a whole day and a half, while the receptionist rudely ignored her and refused to tell her where he was. Eventually her patience ran out, and although she could hardly reach over the reception desk, she grabbed the haughty receptionist by the lapels and whispered terrifying threats into her ear.

Armed with the information she required, and leaving a quivering receptionist behind her, she set off for Renmort pitch and putt golf course, where he was playing in the 'Doctor Mead Annual Charity Tournament', an event well known for raising funds for the homeless. On arrival, she found the head

---

* Scottish slang: an unaffectionate nod of recognition.

greenkeeper who informed her that he was out on the last fairway with his cronies, and wouldn't be back for at least half an hour. She could tell by his tone that he was not over fond of Doctor Mead and he didn't need much encouragement to spill the beans: "He's been running this so-called charity event for years," he sniffed. "I've seen it all, and kept quiet to my shame, but what I have never seen, is even a cent ending up in the pockets of those who are in dire need. I witness big slap-up dinners each year with the finest champagne, cigars, limos, large hotel bills and all, but never a homeless person coming forward to receive any charitable donation."

"I heard him last night by the gents' loos, out of the corner of my eye. He had his arm round his lawyer friend; they were as full as a shuck trying to keep each other from falling over. He pretended to be tearful, complaining that it was such a pity that their expenses exceeded their receipts for last year. He boasted that they raised over fifty-five thousand euro, and still managed to show on the books a loss of twelve thousand. He dug his elbow into his lawyer's ribs and winked, then slipped a brown-paper envelope into his inside pocket. He then insisted that he made sure that he got it back as a tax credit. Then they burst out laughing like greedy hyenas and staggered back to the champagne tent to meet the scantily clad hostesses they had specially flown in from Eastern Europe."

Eva had the measure of Doctor Mead and headed immediately home to work out a plan of lethal justice in

Eva and Icarus

43

the style of Atilla the Hun. All of her life she had witnessed such behaviour by those in positions of authority taking advantage of the vulnerable. She despised it: "Some rob you with a six-gun, some with a fountain pen," she cursed, quoting some American folksong she heard back in the sixties. For Eva, this was personal. All of the past miscarriages of justice that she had to endure had come flooding back and were burning inside of her.

Eva was in her mid-forties and as fit as a fiddle, and she ped-dled furiously like a banshee.* "He'll be shitting feckin' great boulders, not just bricks when I get hold of him," she growled.

When she arrived back home, she found Icarus sitting at the breakfast table with a relaxed look of contentment on his face. She smiled in response, not wanting to spoil his happiness by telling him about Doctor Mead.

"I know exactly what I want to do," he declared. "I've been thinking about it for some time. I read some artbooks and artist magazines when I was in Slack-water House, and yes, I'd like to become an artist... well a performance artist that is. Doctor de Grave said that I was a natural extrovert, and that making an exhibition of myself was my métier whatever the feck that is!"

"I could use my persona of Icarus O'Toole, the incredible naked flying man of Achill, to present my art. There are wonder-ful examples all over the world of art performances and instal-lations: there are dead sheep; preserved sharks in tanks; rotting meat with bluebottles attached; piles of bricks; unmade beds and all kinds of inspirational things. The experts say, that the genius is to be the first person to have thought of it. Well I can do that... and Eva, they sell for feckin' millions! The critics accept now that anything can be art, and art can be anything, and it's passé to show off with draughtsmanship, and because it has been accepted that there's no such thing as talent – that's just elitist – well sign me up! I never could draw a straight line, and in fact, that's now seen as a handicap to true expression."

Eva, was encouraged by his intensity, but cautious, she knew that it would not be as easy as Icarus thought. "You know you'll

---

*   Gaelic: an unaffectionate wild woman not in need of hard cash.

need to get your work accepted, perhaps by an important gallery, and have favourable reviews from the art critics." She did not want to pour cold water onto his idea and added thoughtfully: "You should submit your work to one of the open exhibitions that most Academies have each summer; that would be a start. What do you think you could create?"

Icarus replied with a child-like enthusiasm, "I've been reading about an artist called Piero Manzoni who filled ninety tin-cans with human turds. The art world was stunned: it was valued at one-hundred-thousand euro. What an eejit – I've been flushing thousands down the bog for years! – oh, and he's not the only one, an exciting artist called Chris Offili won a major prize for sticking elephant dung to his work...what a great concept! He had something to say about his African origins apparently. It was such a popular idea, that artists couldn't get hold of the stuff for love nor money, but I've got plenty, Sergeant Fitzdick used to say that I was full of it, and I appreciate that now. I'm going to create an installation that nobody will be able turn their noses up at: 'Poetry in Motion', the ponderous act of turd propulsion into a glass tank with hungry bluebottles in attendance, all set to the music of 'Honkytonk Woman'. I intend to have it filmed in slow motion with close-ups and live-steamed... or is it streamed? I don't feckin' know..."

Eva was both shocked and impressed. "Well, if the others can make a success of it Icarus, why not you?"

"It's called feculent art, that's the technical term, after the feckless feckers that do it I suppose. Eva, could you help me to apply for one of those Arts Council grants, that I saw advertised in the newspaper? My shit comes for free, but the video equipment and other shit is expensive to hire."

Eva tried to put a supportive hand on his shoulder but had to settle on squeezing his bony elbow. "It'll be a pleasure," she smiled. "I'll organise the application forms in the morning."

Icarus enthusiastically began sketching out his plans on the back of an old cereal box, and Eva took a measured intake of breath, realising that Icarus's reintroduction to the world he left some ten years ago was not going to be straightforward. If he didn't fit in then, what chance would he have now? He seemed to have none of the normal boundaries of polite behaviour and his colourful language could be so readily misunderstood. "Oh bollix, feck, arseholes and twats!" she whispered to herself.

The next morning, they were out and about early. Eva wanted to treat Icarus and take him on a boat trip into Dingle Bay to see a tame dolphin called Fungie. "He's an old boy now," she remarked, "but creatures of the sea are calming for the soul."

Icarus was very keen to go, he had lived by the ocean for most of his childhood and he had missed it. He had often seen dolphins swimming out beyond the cliffs, and he loved to watch the whales that majestically drifted by most summers.

Eva, bought them both a ticket for the twelve o'clock trip and they waited at the harbour wall as the other ticket holders began to gather. The sea breeze began to pick up, and the man in charge, Captain Colcannon, warned them that they may be in for a bit of 'rock and roll' when they got out to sea. They all scrambled aboard and the Captain produced his squeezebox for later. He liked to entertain his passengers, especially on days when Fungie proved to be elusive, and true to form it proved to be a very boring blank day. After nearly four hours of pitching up and down with white knuckles and feeling queasy, tempers began to fray.

One old lady piped up, "Now I remember why I don't like boats – it's just like sex with my old man: I'm either bored out of my mind or absolutely terrified!" The whole group burst out laughing, apart from Icarus who was wondering yet again what sex were. Eva was totally out of patience and began wittering about a refund when Captain Colcannon suddenly struck up with his Celtic version of 'Jailhouse Rock'. The boat was really rocking and rolling, when suddenly, like a greyhound out of a trap Eva sprang to her feet. She was truly inspired, and began to jive and shake her hips like a banshee,* Icarus, equally excited, immediately joined in. He wasn't familiar with the steps, but boy could he move. They spun each other around, kicked and flicked out their feet with elbows and knees going in all directions and

---

* Gaelic: a terrifying crazy woman, often chucked out of pubs and discos.

scared half to death the others in the boat. Unbeknown to each other they both loved to dance. Eva was the current under six-ty-five jive-champion of Tarwathie, the place in Scotland where she was born, and Icarus had been the main cabaret attraction at the Slack-water House Christmas show, with his unique and completely uninhibited dance routine.

"Mammy, I want to go home," cried one little girl. "So do I mammy," agreed Mr Tóibín, the local councillor, who had taken his aging mother out for a special birthday trip. The Captain was having the time of his life, for he had never known such an audi-ence. He skilfully steered the boat with his knees as he waved his squeezebox in the air, completely forgetting about Fungie, who popped his head out off the water and squeaked at them. Nobody noticed him, so he just slipped away sulking. Apparently, that's what dolphins do when ignored.

The brisk breeze had developed into quite a gale, and Captain Colcannon thought it best to return back to shore and safety. The passengers shouted out demanding a full refund, all except the councillor's ninety-three-year-old mother, whose flailing arms and pulsating torso had to be pinned down to her seat, as the dancing fired up passions in her, long thought to be extinguished.

"That was a blast," grinned Icarus as he disembarked. "So it was," agreed Eva, "how we managed not to fall in, I'll never know." They were followed by the Captain, who picked up his playing again.

This time he joined in with the dancing, and the little old lady who had been met by a wheel chair and nurse from the old folks' home, refused to be restrained. She smacked the nurse and her son on the head with her brolly and joined in with a youthful joy to the dulcet tones and throbbing beat of 'I Want to Break Free'.

Very soon a delighted crowd gathered and began to throw money into the cap that had been strategically positioned on the ground by the Captain. In less than half an hour they had taken over a hundred euro, but It all came to an abrupt end when Councillor Tóibín returned with a Garda and a doctor carry-ing an oxygen bottle and mask for his mother. She gave her son a smart kick in the arse of his pants for spoiling her fun, then lunged forward to berate the Garda with her brolly. He threatened to arrest them all for a public disturbance violation, and to lock them up and throw away the key if they didn't calm down. Her long-suffering son, slowly slumped to the ground, and with shaking hands tried to reach for the oxygen mask himself.

After the crowd dispersed, Captain Colcannon shared out the spoils. "Ten feckin' euro?" Eva protested, "Ye cheating bollix of a *sleeveen*,* that's not even the cost of one of your tickets!"

"Ah, but it's my boat, and I provided the music," he declared.

"And what about the granny; what did you pay her?"

"Oh, she was so delighted, she gave me a fifty-euro tip," he gloated.

Icarus regardless was thrilled, "Performance art is the way to go," he whooped... "feckin' superb slapped pink buttocks of a day!"

Eva was still outraged for she understood well the pitfalls and trials of artistic endeavour, and how artists are so easily exploited. "Let's go home," she sighed, "we have a lot to talk about and I've had a lamb stew in the oven since this morning which I'm looking forward to... oh, and yes, the Arts Council grant form came in the post this morning. We need to fill it in."

Icarus stretched his overlong legs onto Eva's floor-cushion and asked to see the application form. "There's a questionnaire included here, asking all kinds of personal stuff," he shouted.

Eva was dishing out the stew and casually shouted back: "Don't worry about that, it's all about political correctness, it's a kind of survey that's supposed to free us all up and make the world a better place. Put down the first thing that comes into your head, I always do."

Icarus replied, "They seem obsessed with something I haven't a clue about: am I a surviving partner from a same-sex civil partnership legally dissolved; am I bisexual, gay, straight, trans... something or other. What's all that about Eva? And they want to know which group I consider I belong to: White, Chinese, Indian, Pakistani, Irish Traveller, black African, black Caribbean,

---

* Irish slang: a smooth-tongued chancer; an opportunistic twat.

black other... black other what, for feck's sake? I'd like to join them all if they'll have me... it sounds great...! And what's this...? What denomination do I belong to? – I think I'll score top marks on this question; we talked about this in our group sessions in Slack-water House. Mrs Evans apologised and confessed she was C of E, and hoped her being a member of the Church of Egypt didn't offend anyone. Mr McTweezer said he was a fully paid-up member of the Jedi Temple and we should all feck off, and I was told I was a Roaming Catholic, so that's my answer, bit like being a wandering Jew I guess."

"And what are these things called sex? Doctor de Grave was going to tell me one day, but he never did and I've forgotten all about it. Mr McTweezer once asked me if I was a boy or a girl or an inbetweeny, but he used to ask me all kinds of weird things. I think it was his medication talking, plus the naggin of whiskey he washed it all down with. Does any of this matter Eva?" asked Icarus, "It's enough to put you off applying altogether."

"Just do your best," replied Eva with a smile, "it's all anyone can do." She called Icarus to sit down at the table and she dished out the lamb stew. It smelled delicious and they were both very hungry. "Tuck in my boy, a tractor won't run without diesel, and after our merry dance – it was the dog's bollocks* wasn't it? – we need to refuel."

Over dinner, Eva asked what he could remember about his little cottage. "Very little," he replied. "I remember those terrible headaches and awful pains in my bones. I had strange but lovely dreams about a pretty little girl with a wonderful smile, and I used to wake up each morning to what looked like an angel holding my hand, but I guess that I was still dreaming. She always kissed me each day before she vanished, and eventually she disappeared for good and I never saw her again. The pain was bearable when she held my hand, but terrible when I was alone."

Eva opened Icarus's file and took out a photograph which she placed in his hand. "Was this your angel?" she asked. Icarus's eyes

---

*   Anglo Saxon: outstanding like a dog's testicles – worthy of being licked!

filled with tears. "That's Mary O'Toole, your loving mother. She was your guardian angel for those long dark months."

"I thought it was just a dream," he sighed. "Where is she now? I'd like to see her now I'm well again."

Eva could hardly bring herself to tell him of his loss. It could have been the straw that breaks the camel's back. "I'm so, so sorry," she replied, "she died over ten years ago. When the doctor found her, she was by your bedside holding on to your hand."

"When they came to take her away, the undertakers found it impossible to get you to release your grip even though you were drowsy from the medication. It took two burly farmers and a small crowbar to make you let go. If you examine your left hand, you can still see the marks."

Icarus looked at his hand; he felt numb and so he picked up his little dolly that Nurse Bigley's daughter had given him and gave it a cuddle. "Don't worry Daisy," he said, "things will come back to me... Daisy," he wondered silently to himself... "Daisy?"

Icarus pushed his stew away from him and Eva took hold of his hand. It was not the right time to tell him about Daisy Maisie, so she focused on telling him as much as she could about his mammy and their little cottage. He had many questions, many that she could not answer and some she chose not to. Icarus had been told that he had been badly injured after accidentally falling off the high cliffs of Croaghaun, and he had been so ill for such a long time that it had affected his emotional and mental state – hence his stay in Slack-water House. She decided to keep the truth about his horrific beating until another day. She also needed to explain what the feck sex were, but perhaps not until the morning.

"Jaysus!"* she thought to herself, "What the feck have I let myself in for?"

It had been a long day and Eva gave Icarus a hug to say goodnight. Her arms only just reached around him and the top of her head only came up to his navel, but it was a hug of true warmth

* Irish slang: an exclamation of disbelief. A bearded holy *garsún*.

and affection. Icarus bent down and tenderly kissed the top of her head. She could feel his tears fall onto her hair.

"This," she said to herself... "this is what I have let myself in for."

The next morning was dark and miserable. Heavy rain had spread in from the Atlantic and rattled against the window over the breakfast table. Icarus stared at it; he began to picture a broken window that let in the rain, and a newspaper being jammed in the hole by someone – but then it was gone, and so he took a big slurp from his mug of tea.

Icarus spread the application form out over the table before Eva had chance to clear it and she quickly showed her annoyance.

"Hey, what did yer last servant die of?" she said sharply, "You might have been treated like royalty at Slack-water House with kitchen-staff and carers, but if you stay here, you muck in!"

Icarus apologised and started to help, but Eva tutted in annoyance after discovering the application form sticky with marmalade and stained with tea. She snatched the dishes from him and told him to sit down. "Men!" she barked, "They're all feckin' useless."

After five minutes of noisy dish-washing and even noisier curses, Eva came back into the kitchen wearing a smile of appeasement. "Don't mind me," she said. "I'm so used to having to deal with pompous lazy men, who have been promoted well beyond their intellectual capacity, that it has started to affect how I deal with everyone."

"You know my own daddy was as gentle as a lamb. When I became engaged to a ne'er-do-well when I was only sixteen, he tried to talk me out of it in his fatherly way, but I wouldn't listen. When he walked me down the aisle later that year, I know that it broke his heart. I did it just to spite my drunk of a mother who was a real Glaswegian bully, but she couldn't have cared less. It was my daddy I hurt. Later that year he was proved right. The drunken gobshite* put me in hospital after finding out that I was

* Irish slang: an individual of questionable character, best avoided.

pregnant. He said he wasn't the father, but of course he was. I lost that child, and haven't been with a man since – thank God!"

Icarus couldn't remember that he couldn't remember his father, and Eva, seeing his puzzlement, told him the few scraps of information that she had seen in his file. "You know you had a father: of course, everyone has a father of some kind or other. He had a big problem with the drink: he just couldn't get enough of it. He used to work on the fishing boats, but he was sacked, because of his drinking; he kept putting the other fishermen at risk. He fell overboard one day and they nearly lost two of the crew trying to rescue him. Without work the drinking got worse and he got worse. He was always flat broke, but somehow always had money for drink, much to the distress of your mother whom he had promised to marry in sober times."

"He took to smuggling up and down the west coast, and he was very successful at it; too successful in fact as he attracted the beady eye of the Customs and Excise, who went after him in a big way. He was about to beach a huge consignment of Russian Vodka, during a massive autumn storm when he was spotted off Achillbeg Island. A frantic chase ensued involving powerful speedboats and gigantic waves, but the only thing they found was his wrecked empty boat, all smashed up on the slab rocks. Tomás Gogarty, your father is recorded to have been lost at sea, presumed dead... I'm so sorry, Icarus."

"So, there is a chance he could be alive, if they never found a body," replied Icarus.

"Please don't, Icarus. The waves were over thirty feet high. Nothing could have survived that pounding. It had been the worst storm for almost a century. The power of the waves was so immense that the steel rails from the boat were twisted like pipe cleaners. The coastguard searched for months and locals walked the beaches each day for over a year, but to no avail. Please Icarus, do not burden yourself with false hopes, many lives are lost at sea, never to be found."

"Look, let's get to the matter in hand, the arts grant application form. We can discuss the other stuff later." Eva was quietly relieved because she didn't really want to give Icarus a sex lesson.

"Jaysus," she whispered to herself, "I sound like a cougar* at best, or a slapper* at worst!"

"Put down the address here Icarus, you can't get arts grant money without a permanent home, and fill in your full name, date of birth and the rest and let's have a look at the first question."

"Number one: **TITLE OF WORK**," read Icarus, "that's easy; 'Poetry in Motion' – top marks there."

"Number two: **BRIEF DESCRIPTION OF WORK**, including media used and size (dimensions) I've been thinking about this, Eva. 'Poop Art' is my overall description. A fresh, natural look at human plumbing via the shit-chute, with the ecological ethics of blue-bottle recycling, all in 3D slow motion video with sound effects, and accompanied by the Rolling Stones singing 'Honkytonk Woman' if they'll do it – I haven't asked them yet."

"Number three: **APPROXIMATE COST OF PROJECT**. Well the basic materials are cheap enough, but I'll put down the cost of a really good scoff. I'll need to stuff myself to make sure that I can give a good show. I've heard that artists, singers in particular can dry up on stage if they are not well prepared... well not me. I'll have an all-day session in 'The Taste of India' and finish off on the way home with a huge donner kebab, and if the chippy is still open, double fish and chips. The consistency of the living sculpture should be attractively shiny and moist, but firm, not sloppy – I don't want to offend anyone by shoddy workmanship. Anyway, I'll put down one hundred euro for sourcing the material, and five hundred euro for hire of video equipment and lighting etc."

"The Rolling Stones, according to their agents, will be five hundred thousand euro, and with say, five thousand for P.R. and advertising, that should do it nicely. What do you think Eva? Five hundred and five thousand, six hundred euro."

"Sounds good," replied Eva who was starting to worry that it could all get out of hand.

---

*   American terminology: a rather large pussy.

*   Anglo Saxon terminology: an over affectionate woman with a rather large pussy.

"Last part: **MISSION STATEMENT**, core values, target audience, aims and objectives. What the feck does that mean Eva?"

"Oh, that's the bullshit bit Icarus; in modern parlance it's called psycho-babble. Don't be blasé about it though, because that is the most important part about your application, well that and your CV which we'll discuss later. I've observed absolute shite being lauded as great art, with all the critics and their sycophants standing around nodding to each other like those toy dogs you see in the backs of cars, whilst sipping cheap warm Chardonnay. If you want your work to be accepted, pay great attention to that part. Anyway, I'm off into town, I've got a bit of research to do about a doctor who needs my special care and assistance... See ya!"

Icarus sucked hard on his pen, then began to write: 'My work is designed to make feculent art tasteful. I also wish to bring to the masses the dynamic reality of humanity's ecological responsibility of daily deposits combined with the sheer joy and pleasure of a good quality morning-motion. I wish to free us by shining a spotlight on the dark grip of guilt that crushes us all.'

'We hide away in dingy little rooms, trying not to make a sound, and cough or run a tap if we do. To avoid a loud plop, we even lower turds down on sheets of toilet paper as if we should be ashamed. We should be proud of our creations, they are part of us. They are our children, for a while at least and they deserve our love.'

'We deny the truth and make lame excuses, saying that we are doing something else such as 'I'm off to wash my hands before dinner', or 'I'm going to switch off the hot water', and then take twenty minutes before coming back and looking flushed.'

'My intention is to give society back the absolute thrill and uninhibited beauty of our natural selves, in a celebration of the dynamic and fundamental processes that maintain our mental and physical wellbeing. In short: we all do it, so why be embarrassed?'

Eva arrived home just as he was drawing a line under his application. "I've had a good idea Icarus, why not try to raise some sponsorship. If you are not successful with the Arts Council, the money would be useful, you could still go ahead. A famous toilet-paper company such as Andrex might back you. It's not easy for such a company to get good P.R., I think that's why they chose a fluffy white puppy to feature in their ads. They might see the honesty and ironic humour in your artwork and go for it, because it would appeal to the younger generation known as the millennials."

"I'm not so sure," replied Icarus, "I always thought it was really cruel to wipe your arse on a sweet little white puppy."

Eva rolled her eyes to the heavens, "We'd better attend to your C.V. now, so we can get it in the post in the morning."

"I looked up C.V. in your dictionary that I found in the bread-bin of all places. It is Latin meaning 'course of life'. Jaysus, what can I put down? I've been in a nuthouse most of my life, I have not a single qualification, and…"

"Stall the engines, Icarus, did you never read about Van Gogh? You have so much in common apart from your being a bit taller. He spent much of his time in what you call a nut house himself. He was a wonderfully gifted but tortured soul, who devoted his life to his art, but was never able to sell a single painting. Art was never my best subject at school, but I think I read somewhere that he chopped off his mickey* in a moment of madness and sent it gift-wrapped with pink ribbons to his girlfriend. She was very upset because I think she was hoping for earrings. It all ended tragically when he shot himself when was still quite young. During his short life he was often ridiculed and his work was often mocked, but now it sells for many millions. Does his story strike a chord with you Icarus?"

"Feck me Eva, I won't be chopping off my mickey for anyone. It'd be like cutting my nose off to spite my face! But back to matters in hand, what on earth can I write on my C.V.?"

"Well," replied Eva with a tone of defiance, "with a gentle bit of creative embroidering of the truth, and a few mild fibs here and there, together with a bit of outrageous lying, we should be

---

* Irish slang: male member; not a politician nor a Freemason.

okay. Don't worry Icarus, everybody does it, nobody could be bothered checking them anyway."

"You graduated with honours from the École des Faux Arts in French Guyana, just before it was bombed and destroyed by the local rebel militia. You won the prestigious 'Tête de Richard' prize for misconceptual art and macramé, and then you spent the last ten years as artist in residence at Slack-water House specialising in scatological choreography and the troubled colon."

"But you know I never lie," protested Icarus.

"And neither shall you," Eva reassured Icarus. "I'll fill it in and post it. It'll be me who burns in hell!"

Icarus handed the paperwork over to Eva to complete and post, and they decided to go out for a stroll by the sea to freshen up their strained brains. It was a beautiful soft afternoon out by Spanish point where Eva had brought them. The Atlantic was as calm as a sleeping child and shone as blue as a kingfisher's wings. She decided it was opportune to tell Icarus about Doctor Mead, and how she intended to get his cottage back for him and kick him up the arse figuratively speaking and literally at the same time.

Icarus, never ever bore a grudge or ever whinged, but out of character, he became very cross. "He was in no small part to blame for my mother's untimely death then," he snapped as he took hold of Eva by her two arms. "What are we going to do?"

Eva knew that she had to tread carefully. Icarus was a gentle soul that she didn't want to see destroyed by bitterness in the pursuit of revenge; but justice had to be restored. He couldn't stay with her forever, and the next step in his rehabilitation was to become independent.

"I've been doing a bit of research and digging around about Doctor Mead. I know he's not the only one involved, but he's the main man. I spoke to him on the phone yesterday and he revealed his weakness to me. He is supremely arrogant and he doesn't think he has any weaknesses. He is convinced he is much cleverer than anyone around him and together with his bombastic nature, he gets away with murder."

"Everyone is too scared to challenge him. He's also a well-practiced bully, but like all bullies, he is a coward at heart, he feels powerful and enjoys preying on the weak and vulnerable. He was so condescending to me: he told me that the law was far too legal for my female brain to understand, and that I should go home and read my self-help books. You know, you should never give an angry dog a sniff of meat, or in my case an angry bitch!"

Icarus looked down at her diminutive figure yet enormous personality. She was a simmering volcano about to become cataclysmic, and heaven help those caught in the lava flow.

"I did a bit of background checking, Icarus. On his surgery wall he has his medical certificate which states that he qualified in medicine at The Metropolitan Medical College in Chicago. That college closed in nineteen hundred for reasons of fraud, making him at least one hundred and forty years old if he graduated there before it closed. He did work in a few hospitals in the USA, but only as a porter, he must have picked up a few basic skills there and he's been conning people for years. I've written to the Irish Medical Council that has a register for qualified doctors, and when I have their reply, he'll be well and truly banjaxed."*

"I was able to check his property portfolio, those that are on public record at least. He owns eighty-four houses, mostly attained from poor folk who needed to go into a home. He paid them a pittance and made it seem like he was doing them a favour. A neighbour of old Miss Collins told me he paid only two hundred euro for her house that her family had owned from when the Normans first came to Ireland. She could hardly see and thought that the cheque had two more noughts on the amount. She died shortly after with no surviving family to fight her corner, and of course he inherited all of her possessions."

"Rumour has it that he has over three hundred other properties acquired in a similar fashion, unknown to the taxman. I'll enjoy tipping them the wink. Then there's his so-called charity work: it's all a front to launder money from his property scams. He even gets public funding to assist the running of his charity's

---

* Irish slang: well and truly fucked.

administration. The taxpayer pays for bent accountants and lawyers to hike up his costs and hide his profits in overseas accounts. He also has nearly fifty cases of medical malpractice brought against him, but somehow, they all evaporate before reaching any kind of hearing. He's some can of piss that man; he'd steal the eyes right out of yer head if yer weren't looking."

"Anyway, he'll be getting an undie-grundie✳ in public in front of all of his posh friends at his golf club, and more importantly the Gardaí. So, while we wait for your reply from the Arts Council, and my reply from the Medical Council, I suggest we just chillax."

Eva turned to walk back to the road that led them there when Icarus let out an excited whoop. He was already fifty yards away, naked and flapping in all directions and running towards the cliff tops. She turned to follow him and picked up his scattered clothes.

"He'll be needing these," she laughed to herself. "There's a bus load of day-trippers up there – retired nuns from St Vergüenza's Convent... I don't want to miss this!"

Back home, Eva poured them both a refreshing cup of tea from a lovely china teapot that had been her aunty Bridie's. "I love this teapot," she said, "every time I use it I think of her. She was an elegant well-educated woman who loved beautiful things. She was my father's sister, and when I was in trouble – which was often – I always went to her. However frustrated and angry I was, she would always tell me to be true to myself, ignore the criticism of others, and that in my heart, I would know if I was doing wrong or not."

"So, when you stood there on Spanish Point as the incredible naked flying man, still as a Greek statue, with all of those hysterical nuns swooning about the place, did you feel you were doing wrong?"

Icarus thought for a while: "It is always a beautiful thing for me, the invigorating wind, the majestic scenery, the purity of all that is natural. I can't understand why they say I am disgusting

✳ Irish slang: a wedgie – an unexpected vertical tug of the underpants forcing them into the gicker-crack

and filthy; they curse me and say that I am in league with the devil whoever that might be. I think the devil is a disease that dwells in men's hearts: he's not a being, but a corruption that makes people see darkness wherever they look."

"Well said!" agreed Eva with a slap on her thigh. "I hope you speak up with such eloquence at the District Court on Tuesday, you've been charged with four counts of indecent exposure, two counts of performing obscene works, and one of creating mayhem in a public place!"

On the Tuesday morning, before his appearance in the District Court, the letter from the Arts Council arrived. Eva suggested that he should wait until he came back, but he had already torn it open with shaking hands. "You read it Eva," he pleaded, "I'm so excited I'm unable to."

Eva took it purposefully from him and began to read. She looked up at him and said, "I'm so sorry, Icarus, they've rejected your application."

Icarus snatched it back. "It states here that my application was insolent and pretentious and that the administration staff have had to be sent for counselling to cope with the distress of handling such obscene material. They are also considering presenting my application form to the Gardaí for further action."

"Don't take it to heart Icarus, great art is rarely understood. Throughout history, many pioneering thinkers were treated as such. Galileo was kept under house arrest until his death. He offended the Church by daring to say that the planets revolved around the sun and not as they insisted, the other way round."

Icarus looked into the sky, "They think my art stinks, well it may be shite, but I'll show them it's not shit!"

"That's the spirit!" shouted Eva, who went to slap him on the back, but unable to reach clattered his arse in error.

"Woa," shouted Icarus, "you couldn't hit a cow's arse with a banjo!"

Later in the District Court, the haughty Judge Nigel Trimble-bum was eating the head off Icarus: "Now look here Mr O'Toole, we can't have you acting the maggot and scaring people half to death. If we were meant to go around displaying our naked bodies, God would have made it be much warmer outside in Ireland. We also wear clothes out of common decency and that's my last word on the matter. If your social worker hadn't given you such a glowing report, you'd be doing three years in Mountsad prison. You are hereby bound over to keep the peace, or mark my words, you'll rot in Mountsad for sure."

"Thank you sir," replied Icarus, and whispered, "*póg mo thóin!*"*

"What was that?" demanded the judge.

"Thank you sir, and have a pleasant journey home," he replied, quick as a flash.

Back at home later that afternoon, Eva poured out more tea.

"Ah, lovely... comfort juice," smiled Icarus as he slumped back into the easy chair. "But where do I go from here?"

"Whatever you do you'll have to be careful; you've upset the Arts Council, the Gardaí, the retired nuns from St Vergüenza's and the District Judge is just dying for you to make a mistake. I don't think you should give up on your art show however, just be a little more discrete if you can."

"You mean I should excrete and be discreet all in one?" said Icarus with a wry smile. "Shite is right and shite is might!"

"Look I don't want to get your hopes up, but I had a phone call from a toilet-roll company yesterday who were interested in sponsoring your work. They don't know all the details, so let's keep them in the dark a little, we don't want to put them off, and you need the cash. Also, there is a charity shop in town that's recently closed. I'll pretend we want to rent it and I'll get the key. It'll only take an hour or so to set up the cameras and the video link. We'll have to get in the local ceilidh band for the music though. Mick Jagger phoned this morning and confessed that the Stones would have loved to have done the gig, but they've consumed enough shit to last ten lifetimes, and want to put all that behind them."

And so it was; the date for Icarus's art extravaganza was set for two days' time, and Icarus prepared for his big feast by starving himself beforehand. "Jaysus, I could eat a farmer's arse through a

---

*   Gaelic: kiss my ass – not the long-eared quadruped.

blackthorn bush," he declared as he woke up with one day to go. He then dressed quickly and with a growing excitement, scurried off into town.

His first stop was Sean's Diner, where he started slowly with a full-Irish breakfast with half a dozen eggs and ten extra sausages all smothered in brown sauce. At eleven o'clock, just to keep himself going, he had a huge slice of black forest gateau and four brownies with lashings of chocolate and caramel sauce. "Traditional and authentic colouring will be observed in this masterpiece!" he declared like Caravaggio about to start on a new canvas.

He then headed off to the Taste of India for his all-day session and began to work his way through the menu. Icarus loved curries, ever since Naan Bhaaji Singh became a guest at Slack-water House. In 'recreational cookery', he had introduced all kinds of spectacular dishes to inmates and staff alike. He had been valued and much loved by everyone, but in fact no one really knew why he was there. Rumour had it that he had been head-chef in some exotic royal household, but he had been dishonourably expelled. He had fallen in love with the young Prince, and each day they had been secretly slipping marijuana into the curries to keep everyone peaceful and happy. Disaster stuck when they slept in one morning and hadn't time to 'herbalise' the Prince's parents and they were caught lying in each other's arms. Naan Bhaaji Singh only just escaped being beheaded if he accepted deportation and incarceration. As is the way with these things, a huge exchange of cash had found its way into the coffers of Slack-water House, together with generous monthly payments, so long as he remained there.

Icarus waded through a mountain of tikkas, pakoras, biryanis and kormas, and was bursting for the vindaloo. He was a very tall man but skinny and by ten o'clock it looked as though he had swallowed a basketball. Eva called in to see how he was doing and to pick up the bill, and suggested they start to make their way back home.

"But I've two more stops to make," protested Icarus sweating like an overloaded donkey, "Ben Ali's kebab shop and the chippy – if I can get out from under this table."

Somehow, he managed to force down a large donner and almost, but not quite, double fish and chips. He took almost an hour to waddle home like a disorientated duck and had to sleep all night in the easy chair sitting upright. Both he and Eva thought it unwise to put any pressure on his gut.

The ceilidh band had been given very little information – obviously, and had been told to practice 'Honkytonk Woman'. It sounded really very good if not a little bizarre with harp, flute and whistle, and Mrs Collins, the ninety-two-year-old contralto with tambourine attached as lead singer. They really got into it, and even tried 'Paint it Black' and other Rolling Stones classics. They did a surreal version of 'Satisfaction', which had a hypnotic effect on Mrs Collins. She began strutting about like a demented gibbon with ridiculously pursed lips as her stockings slowly slipped down her legs. Alarmingly, she almost choked to death after nearly swallowing her false teeth and was saved just in time by Mr McLiver who was the band's first aider and his eight-year-old son. They both grabbed her, and his son who had smaller hands, stuffed his fingers down her throat to hook out her dislodged teeth. All the while she was gurgling the words "I can't get no…" as she bashed Mr McLiver on the head with her tambourine in perfect rhythm.

Mr McLiver's son was still holding her dripping false teeth that hadn't been brushed properly in years and still held the residue of her full Irish breakfast. He squeamishly handed them over to his father and rushed into the toilet 'to call for O'Rourke'.✱

On the morning of the 'Poetry in Motion' performance, as the flyers described it, Eva handed all of her information about Doctor Mead to the Gardaí and the Tax Office. She smiled in satisfaction as she went down to the old charity shop in the town to let in the sound and video technicians, and of course Icarus.

✱   Onomatopoeic: self-explanatory.

He had been hyped up and waiting outside since six thirty, too excited to have breakfast. He was dressed in a second-hand flowery silk full-length dressing gown which struggled to reach below his crotch, and the flimsy tie which should have been around his middle, was actually knotted just below his armpits and burst open at every opportunity. Modesty had never been a hindrance to Icarus, and he unselfishly shared his undercarriage with his every bend and turn, as they loaded and installed each piece of equipment.

The previous day's feasting had gone well to plan, having stuffed himself almost to bursting, and apart from flashing his co-workers, he shared the ghastly gaseous aftermath both anally and orally: "Just a little taste of what's to follow!" he burped with pride.

Standing in the doorframe were the arts correspondent for the Times, and some cynical red-top hack who had come along for a laugh. "Going for the Turder Prize?" he mocked as he waved the flier. "I see you're starting with a smear campaign!"

"Gangway!" shouted Eva, as she trolleyed in the aquarium that would be the 'focal or faecal-point' as the flier described for the video link. She tossed in a handful of maggots that she had bought at the fishing-tackle shop, made some minor adjustments, winked at Icarus and said, "Whenever you're ready."

Icarus however was slumped against the wall, white as a sheet, and moaning and gurgling from every orifice. "Jaysus!" he groaned, "That last donner was a bit iffy, I'm fair touchin' cloth!"

"What's the aquarium for?" demanded the hack in an insolent way.

"It's for the containment and display of the brown trout," groaned Icarus as he attempted to make ready.

'Poetry in Motion' had been billed to start at eleven in the morning sharp, and it had caught everyone's imagination and curiosity. By ten-thirty, the small ex-charity shop was packed to the gills. No one really knew what to expect, and as soon as the ceilidh band arrived they were asked by Eva to start playing. Councillor Tóibín's ninety-three-year-old mother turned up by taxi and immediately got everyone up to dance. She radiated the smile of a six-year-old innocent, absolutely clueless to the mayhem and chaos that was about to begin.

The stage was set: cameras in place, strobe lighting flashing with a rousing ceilidh version of 'Honkytonk Woman' screaming out over the loudspeakers that the local electrical shop had installed for free. The band had been augmented by three Lambeg drums, sent by the Arts Council down from Belfast to help promote closeness between the North and the Republic, and every diddley-eye musician, good, bad or rubbish from miles around came for their moment in the sun. The din was unbelievable.

Mrs Collins had been practicing with such unrestrained enthusiasm, that her voice was shot and she sounded like a callously kicked mule. In the strobe lighting, she did not notice that Eva had handed her a cucumber in place of her microphone and she continued to rave like a Rockstar on speed. Eva took the real microphone and sang herself, not really knowing the words as a confused Mrs Collins constantly tapped her cucumber and felt for the on off switch.

By eleven o'clock there was such a crowd on the pavement outside, that the Gardaí arrived and started putting up cordons. The Fire-Service was also called as were several St John's ambulances, and confusion reigned supremely.

Icarus, by that time was feeling very ill and with his bowels fit to burst, he could contain his performance no longer. The aquarium had been positioned in the shop window for full panoramic audience viewing, and Icarus dropped his dressing gown and struck up his pose. He began to lower himself into his delivery position when a tidal wave of Gardaí Síochána came crashing in through the door.

"Stop that man!" bellowed the sergeant as twenty burly Gardaí bundled people out of the way and tried to throw a blanket over his naked body. The jostling was far too much for his overstretched personal plumbing, and the resulting explosion spared neither saint nor sinner. Two police dogs ran away yelping with their tails between their legs dragging their skidding handlers behind them. The mess was devastating, and the lady representing the toilet-roll company tore up the sponsorship cheque in

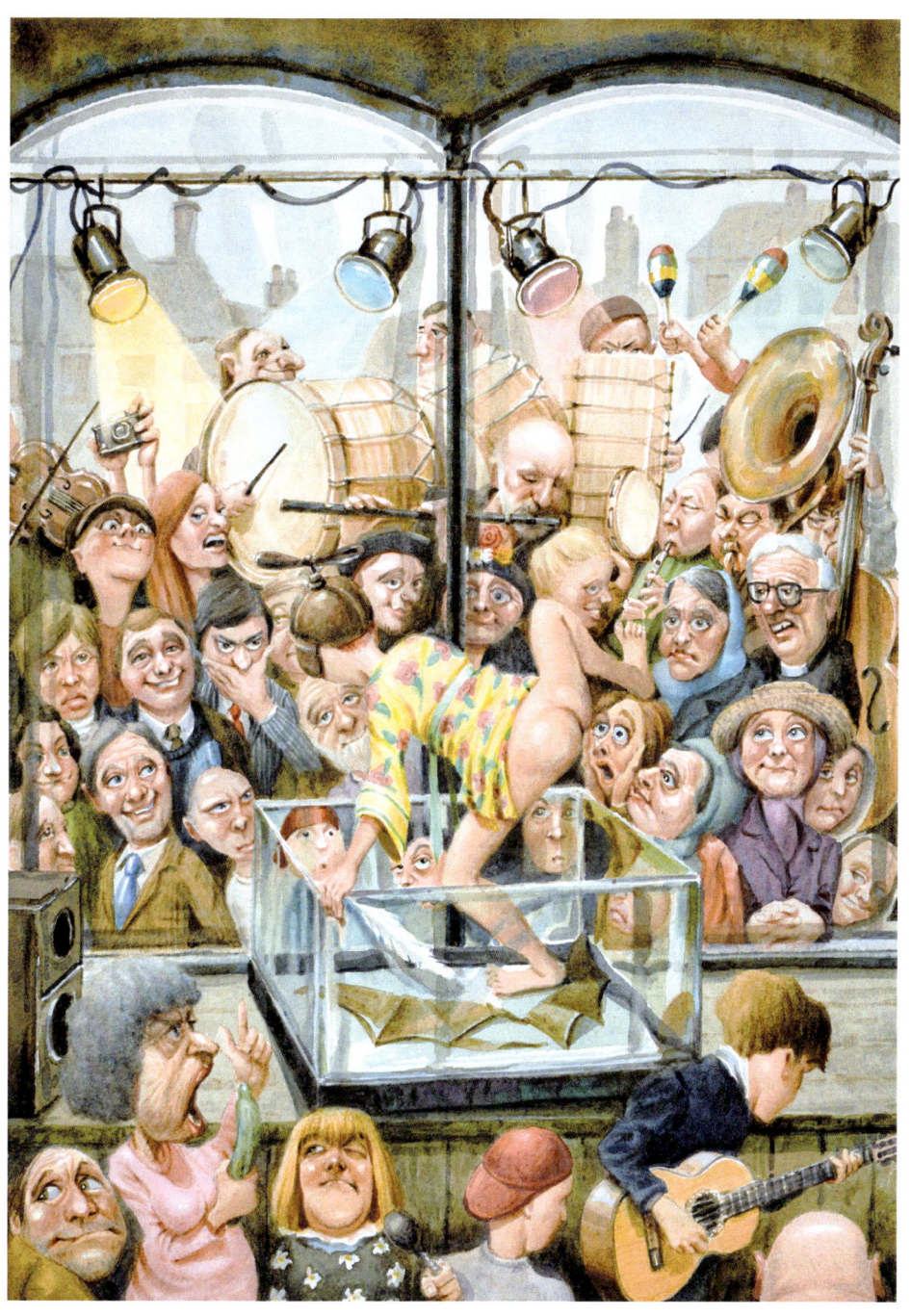

'Poetry in Motion'

disgust. She still had the presence of mind however, to sell her free samples at outrageous prices to the splattered audience.

Icarus was restrained and led away through the soggy crowd. Only one man cheered; Mr McTweezer who had been allowed out as a special concession to see his dear friend: "Bra-feckin'-vis-simo, Icarus," he shouted like a crazed football fan at the GAA final in Croke Park. "Truth will always triumph; cream always floats on top... as do turds for that matter! Mind you, my bad boys have been sinking since they put me on that new high-octane diet with..."

"Come along now," interrupted Doctor de Grave, "show's over."

Icarus, slippery as an eel, squirmed and wriggled as they tried to secure him. He remembered with great anguish the last time he was led away in such fashion, but defiantly cried out with pride: "All in the name of art," as he slipped free and speedily squelched for the hills.

"I've made my skid-mark in the anals of fine art!"

"I think I'll hire him for next spring," remarked farmer Flynn, "that's one hell of a muck spreader!"

THE FLIGHT OF ICARUS

HE VERY NEXT DAY the headlines in The Wild Atlantic Times read: 'BIRDMAN FLEES, GARDAI IN A FLAP.' It continued: 'Dangerous birdman gives the Gardaí the slip. Yesterday morning, alleged notorious pervert Timmy O'Toole, alias Icarus O'Toole escaped after being detained at the unveiling of his obscene art-installation entitled: 'Poetry in Motion'. The public are being warned not to approach the highly dangerous fugitive, who had recently been released from Slack-water House, detention centre for the emotionally and mentally deranged. He was last seen heading in the direction of Macbillygoat's Reeks, naked apart from a pair of leather wings strapped to his shoulders and arms. He was also wearing some kind of leather flying-man's cap with a whirligig attached and sporting a white scarf. He also had a large white feather poking out between his buttocks in a most loathsome act of defiance. Councillor Tóibín declared that it was a disgrace that the good name of Dingle had been dangled in the dirt and that the person who allowed the debacle to happen should be severely disciplined...'

"Dearie me, oh dear, oh dear oh dear," sighed Eva as she folded the newspaper over her knee. She was terribly worried for Icarus whom she was still responsible for. She had witnessed his escape and secretly cheered him on as he easily skidded past the Gardaí with his enormous stride. She feared, however, that they would eventually catch up with him, and that they might do him serious harm if and when they did.

Suddenly there was an enormous bang on the door which burst open with a gaggle of Gardaí tangled and fighting over each other to be the first in. They were followed in by Mrs Tapenade, Eva's boss and head social worker and Ms Kapok, the head arts officer from the council. They both swanned in with an arrogance only given those whose self-importance vastly outweighs their capabilities.

Mrs Tapenade tutted as she slid a gloved finger over Eva's sideboard and showed the dust to Ms Kapok. "You were given a position of trust Ms Caber," she said with an expression as if she was smelling something nasty. "A simple task to oversee a troubled individual's reintroduction into society. I made it clear in writing to you that this was to be your last chance. You have let yourself down, Mr O'Toole down, and most unforgivably, the Department of Social Care down. You are to be suspended forthwith, pending an enquiry and oh yes... you must have no further contact whatsoever with Mr O'Toole."

"Furthermore, you must not make any contact with Doctor Mead, who for some kind of personal vendetta, you have been trying to bring into disrepute. I'll have you know that he is a personal friend of mine and a great supporter of the work done at Slack-water House. From all over Ireland he generously accepts many helpless old folks, who have gone a bit gaga and have had trouble holding on to their homes. He's up for a National Civic award I'll have you know."

"You are trouble Eva Caber, ever since God knows how you managed to find a position as a social worker on our team. I must have been on holiday during the interviews. You also owe Ms Kapok here an apology. I have naturally already done so on behalf of the department, but really Eva..."

"I can speak for myself," interrupted Ms Kapok: "It's mavericks like you who ruin the Arts for the rest of us. They are called Fine Arts for that very reason, because they are refined and sophisticated, not rough and common. We shouldn't be having to put up with your uninformed and filthy opinion of what art is, and dragging us into the mire. My staff are still in shock after Mr O'Toole's application which I know you oversaw. Mrs Tapenade says it had your stamp all over it: I say your dirty paw marks."

"The Arts are for the sensitive amongst us. Standards of intellectual integrity must be maintained and safeguarded. It's not for the dregs of society to contaminate and corrupt what is in essence the highest ethos of the most elite nobility of creativity."

"Bollox, you feckin' supercilious gobshites," barked Eva as she made a dash for the door, "It's no wonder you point your noses in the air, it's for fear of smelling your own shite!"

Eva was roughly pounced on by the Gardaí before she could make her escape. They struggled hard to subdue her Glaswegian fury, as her arms and legs flailed furiously like an out of control windmill in a gale. Her teeth snapped like an alligator and her head butted like a mountain goat in the rutting season. It took each and every Gardaí using all of their might to pin her down: "Eva Caber," gasped the sergeant exhausted and sweating: "I'm arresting you for resisting arrest; incitement to public affray; offences against the obscenities act; encouraging and assisting a fugitive; and deformation of character."

As they bundled her out of her flat, Mrs Tapenade and Ms Kapok followed her out into the street. The air was purple with a terrible cursing, and they both nodded to each

- Mrs Tapenade & Ms Kapok -

69

other in self-congratulatory smugness as self-appointed guardians of polite society.

Behind them, Doctor Mead – who had agents and spies all down the west coast – scurried like a rodent into Eva's flat wearing a nasty little grin. He produced a tape measure from his back pocket, licked his pencil with relish and began to jot down notes.

Icarus spent an uneasy night hiding in the mountains and he was freezing cold. He tried to keep warm by jogging and was almost at the summit of Carrauntoohil, Ireland's highest peak. He had been able to see it every day from his window at Slack-water House, except when it was covered in cloud, as it was on that day.

He stumbled and fought his way through the chilling mists and harsh terrain, safely obscured from the chasing pack, who unwittingly were scaling an adjacent peak, some five miles away. Icarus intended to soar as the Incredible Naked Flying Man of Achill, high into the sky, before he was taken away and locked up as he knew would be his fate. On the very highest outcrop of rock, he smoothed out his arse-rudder feather and stretched himself up to his maximum height. He opened his wings like a magnificent Inca god, closed his eyes and released his imagination as high as it would fly – just as the mist swirled and swallowed him up again.

Eventually as if by divine intervention, the mist partially cleared and a sword of sunlight pierced the mirk and illuminated him from above. It was mysterious and beautiful and deeply spiritual. As the mist cleared further, a group of forty Japanese tourists who had been hidden and unknowingly sharing the summit slowly materialised. They felt certain that they were being treated to something very special. "Gaeric tladition!" they deduced as they applauded wildly, as they placed dozens of euro notes into the small knapsack he had dropped by his feet. "Like Finn McCool!" they cooed enthusiastically as they snapped hundreds of photos, "Except with big *hane**＊** stuck in *ketsu no ana**＊*!"

Icarus remained motionless, eyes tightly shut; he was circling over the pyramids of Giza once more and flying with the swallows

---

＊ Japanese: feather
＊ Japanese: arsehole.

on their way back to warmer climes. He could see a beautiful green meadow in the distance and a girl with a beautiful smile holding out to him a white necklace, when his dream was pierced by the shriek of a hunting horn.

Eventually, the clearing mist revealed his sculptural form to the chasing pack and they were soon to be upon him. Icarus, didn't care and he was totally oblivious to it because he yearned to fly again and find the enchanting smiling girl. He closed his eyes tightly once more, when out of the blue he felt a sharp tug on his elbow.

"Come with me," a reassuring voice bade him as the mist closed in again, and he was gently led away into a well-hidden narrow ravine to safety by someone he could not really see. Icarus thought he could just make out a man dressed in black with a white collar, but he could not be sure. He sat there peacefully and perfectly concealed for at least an hour as he heard the posse pass by in the opposite direction. They were banging pans and dustbin lids with shillelaghs and shouting and hollering as if they were hunting a dumb animal.

He hadn't a clue where his rescuer had disappeared to, and as the mist gradually then completely cleared, he found by his side a bundle of clothes – surprisingly in his size; food and drink and money, and Daisy his little dolly. Further down the ravine tumbled a crystal-clear mountain stream which he waded into and washed the filth from his body that had adorned him for the past two days. The cool water also cleared the mush that was in his head, and gently soothed the pain that was in his soul.

He dressed himself in the smart green corduroy suit that had been left him, and pulled on the huge Doc Martin boots and tied them up. He felt great: "New pants, new day, fresh start!" He smiled brightly, for he was not a man to sulk.

He could feel something in his trouser pocket and fumbled around, and eventually pulled out an envelope. He very gently opened it and slid out a folded piece of paper which contained a circle of pressed flowers. It was the daisy chain that Daisy Maisie had lovingly placed about his neck when they were children. He stared at it for ages but could not for the life of him fathom out its significance. His eyes filled with tears of frustration and he carefully put it back into the envelope and tucked it into his pocket. He picked up his little dolly and gave it a kiss: "Come on Daisy, let's go," he sighed, and headed down to the valley below, glad that no one had seen him. "Jaysus... kissing dollies at my age," he puffed.

Icarus was very aware that he was a fugitive from the law and that he would have to be very careful. Trying to be inconspicuous at six feet ten was not going to be easy. Even buying a few bits to eat at a local shop was going to be a risk. "Bollix!" he declared, "If they're going to be chasing me, I'm going to have some fun, what do I have to lose?"

Icarus made his way towards Killarney, feeling that it would be easier to blend into a large town. He pinched a horse-blanket that he found draped over a hedge and wrapped it round his shoulders like an overcoat. It was a bit tattered and whiffy, but it was a good disguise. When he dipped his knees, he was able to reduce his height by a good six inches, all hidden by the blanket, but it made his gait look rather strange, and walking for any length of time was very wearisome on his legs.

By the time he reached the post office in Muckross, his thighs were burning and he was puffing like a steam-train. When he asked the shopkeeper for a packet of biscuits and a pint of milk, she looked at him with trepidation and called for her partner, who stepped in smartly through door curtain behind the counter.

"And what kind of biscuits would you be requiring sir?" inquired her partner Dolores McWaggon, "Digestives, bourbons, or perhaps you'd prefer cream puffs?"

"Do you have ginger nuts?" replied Icarus in all innocence.

"That's a rather personal question," she replied trying to muffle her laughter. "Come in the back room and we'll have a look."

Icarus was beginning to feel uncomfortable and downright suspicious when the couple came from behind the counter, took him by his enormous hands and led him through into their lounge, as his worn-out legs began to buckle under him.

Sitting there with his tatty little suitcase and an enormous grin on her face was Eva who jumped up to give him a huge hug.

"How the feck did you know I'd be here?" said Icarus in an astonished tone.

"Well Dolores and Suzie McWaggon have been my best friends since our student days, and as I knew you were somewhere in the area, I phoned them and asked them to keep an eye out for you. They heard the chasing party on the hills, and being keen walkers, they went to see what the commotion was all about. They spotted you through their birdwatching binoculars and I guessed you might be looking to buy a few bits and pieces, so I whizzed over here on my trusty bike; easy-peasy really."

Icarus slipped off his smelly horse-blanket and like a newly born fawn, he wobbled as he strained to stand up to his full height. Sporting his smart green suit, he asked, "Would you know anything about the person who gave this to me? I couldn't quite make him out – at least I think it was a him – in the mist."

"You mist him then?" giggled Eva.

"Not the foggiest then?" replied Icarus quick as a flash.

"No, it's all a bit hazy to me."

"Nebulous then?"

"Oh enough, enough," laughed Eva.

"I'll have you know I'm a practitioner of nephology, according to Doctor de Grave," declared Icarus with pride.

"Jaysus!" replied Dolores, "Don't be saying that, you could be in trouble if anyone finds out."

"What for having dodgy kidneys?" said Eva.

"No, for communicating with the dead – like a sorcerer, and other things far too disturbing to mention."

"No, no, no," giggled Icarus in his defence, "I live with my head in the clouds, from the Greek word nephos meaning cloud. But seriously, back to my question, who is it that keeps stepping out of the shadows and helping me? It's all very mysterious."

Eva had her own ideas and told him that in his file, there was a reference to a benefactor who had paid the substantial fees for his treatment at Slack-water House. "Anonymity was insisted upon and it was never challenged as the monies were always paid on time and without fail. Some of the staff thought it was some kind of billionaire philanthropist, and others reckoned on a charitable trust that was made up of donors who had made their money in suspicious ways and were now seeking redemption."

"Mr McTweezer's fees were also paid as were several others. He had a furious barney one Friday because he insisted that the sugarplum fairy paid his fees, and not King Henry the Eighth as his co-patients contended. He called them stupid gickers, because King Henry had his head chopped off by one of his wives at least twelve months back!"

"But the urgent matter in hand is, what are we going to do now? I'm under suspension, I can't go back home until the Gardaí have finished searching for evidence, and you Icarus are a fugitive from the law!"

"I like being on the run," proclaimed Icarus defiantly, "and I fully intend to have lots of fun. I'll sneak about after dark like a creature of the night, and when day breaks, my new art will be revealed. I'll make unexpected public appearances in all kinds of unsuspected places: tops of public buildings, monuments, tall trees, windmills, transmission towers; the possibilities are endless. Each appearance will be a statement about my free art. Free, not just in monetary terms, but also free in thought. I'll leak it to the press that I can be seen at some place or other and then appear somewhere completely different."

"I'll become living works of art, vying with the 'Spire' in Dublin, or the 'Angel of the North' in England. I'll be a new 'Statue of Liberty', living and breathing, or perhaps I'll become Rodin's 'Thinker', naked of course as in the original... the list goes on and on. And when the authorities get wind of my installations, I'll vanish like a spectre, leaving just an artful energy, a ghostly presence in my wake, like a fart in a trance, or in the case of the Mona Lisa, a tart in a France!!"

The three girls giggled, but worried that his plans were more than a bit on the daft side, and although cautious at first in regards to the practicalities and obvious pitfalls, they began to get excited. Icarus's enthusiasm was as catching as a custard pie in the face. Eva spoke first: "I don't want to pour cold water onto your plans, but how are you going to live? You'll need food and shelter, and if you are spotted anywhere – well there are always nasty begrudgers who would delight in dobbing you in – those nasty do-gooders would have you locked up forever and a day, and we don't want to do a stretch either for aiding and abetting."

"I have a sister still living in Tarwathie in Scotland. You should go there and lie low for a while. It is remote, and no one will think of looking for you there and you will be completely unknown. You could take the time to work out your installations in more careful detail and relax and enjoy the beautiful surroundings; just 'til the dust settles. Then when they least expect it, and you are fully prepared, dazzle them like a mighty solar flare!"

Just then the doorbell tinkled in the shop and Suzie pressed an urgent finger to her lips. They all fell silent as she and Dolores ducked through the curtain and stood behind the counter. Flicking through the magazines was Shay Monhue, the cynical investigative hack who had been present at the launch of 'Poetry in Motion'. "I see Eva Caber's bike is outside," he said without looking up.

"What bike is that, and who wants to know?" demanded Dolores as she lifted the magazines from his grubby small hands. "If you've soiled them, you've bought 'em!" she insisted.

He fumbled about in the inside pocket of his raincoat that was years overdue an appointment at the dry-cleaners and handed her his business card. "Don't mind me, I'm not digging, just sifting... something is weird here, I can sniff out a story from miles away. Call me on that number if you get wind of Icarus O'Toole, I'd like to help him if I can... but I want exclusive rights, and of course there'll be a little something in it for you." With that he winked and slid backwards out of the shop.

Eva poked her head gingerly round the curtain: "What the feck did that slimy git want?" she asked, as she examined his card. "Shay Monhue, Sub-editor, *Irish Daily Giobal.*✻ That bollix was at Icarus's show, taking the piss he was... mind you, by the end he was taking a very different bodily expulsion, covered in shite from head to foot he was."

<hr>

✻   Gaelic: rag.

"The dirty fecker," shouted Dolores, "I don't think he's washed his hands since by the state of these magazines!" and she ran outside to see if she could catch him, but he was nowhere to be seen. "You owe me twelve yoyo yer putrid ponce," she shrieked on the top of her voice down the street.

"Not you, Mr Down," she whispered apologetically as the startled octogenarian catapulted out of his Zimmer-frame as he turned the corner to enter the shop and pay for his daily newspaper.

Icarus heard the crash and rushed forward to pick him up. "Am I dead?" he asked Icarus as he stared up at his towering figure, fearing that he was with one of the angels who guarded the pearly gates. "You're fine," Icarus replied, "but you had better come in and sit a while."

Old Mr Down was helped tenderly into the shop's solitary chair, provided for such occasions by the three ladies, fussing round him with a warmth unique to Irish women and mammies. They insisted on offering him a cup of tea as Icarus tried to remove the kinks from his injured Zimmer-frame.

"I know you... at least I recognise you from the newspapers," retorted Mr Down. "You're the young garsún that made a mess of the Gardaí... fan-feckin'-tastic! And those other stuck up arseholes... well done I say... bravo! Pity about the musicians, but hey-ho... collateral damage, it's inevitable in desperate times." He shook Icarus warmly by the hand. "How can I help?"

Eva thanked Mr Down and noted, "If the hack is so quickly on our trail, the Gardaí can't be far behind. We'd better get moving right away. I'll arrange things with my sister in Tarwathie. There are plenty of ferries from Larne to Stranraer, but we won't get one today, and we'll have to smuggle him up north."

"I can help you there," declared old Mr Down. "I am Douglas Down – Doug for short, of Down's Funeral Homes. We will be heading to the north to collect Mr Barrage, who died yesterday. We have to bring him back to his family home for embalming and of course for the funeral.

We'll be driving up an empty coffin in our respectful hearse..."

"Oh no, no, no," interrupted Icarus, "I'm not travelling for hours cooped up in a dead man's box; that's far too weird, even for me. And how do you expect me to breathe with the lid screwed down, and supposing I need an Ertha Kitt* or a hit and miss* on the way? Bollix – I'll take my chances on the bus!"

"Hold on young fella; desperate times require desperate measures. No one ever suspects coffins and hearses; we've made a fortune smuggling goods in from the north, without ever being challenged. People are frightened by corpses and wouldn't be seen dead looking into a coffin. No need to worry about fresh air either, all of our coffins meet modern European standards that ensure if a dead man decides to wake up, we have included ventilation tubes. As far as going to the toilet, you'll just have to hang on: just do the opposite of your 'Poetry in Motion' display."

Icarus was not convinced. "Look I'm six feet ten, and I bet your coffin is a lot shorter than that."

"That's true, but Mr Barrage weighed twenty-two stone. The coffin was tailor-made for him and is very deep and wide. You could lie back with your knees bent and the lid would fit nicely."

Eva interjected, "I think that's a plan Icarus, it sounds foolproof," and before he could protest further, the arrangements were being sorted out with the intention to set off at dawn and catch the midday sailing to Stranraer. Icarus and Eva sat together in the small lounge of the shop. They had enjoyed a light supper together with Dolores and Suzie who had turned in early in preparation for the morning.

"I might not see you for a while Icarus, and there is something important that I have to tell you, something that should have been explained to you when you were a boy. I feel a bit embarrassed discussing it with you now, as you are a grown man, but I see it as my duty."

"You have asked me more than once what sex were, so now I am going to tell you: Sex is the physical expression of love, it is beautiful – not dirty and evil as many will tell you. It is as natural

---

* Cockney rhyming slang: disrespectful use of a charming nightclub singer's name.
* Cockney rhyming slang: taking a piss.

as a daisy in the grass, but mankind, not wanting to be reminded of his animal instincts and bestial origins, and also for reasons of guilt, has often sought to hide this part of himself in a dark place. Anyone living and loving in an open and expressive way, has on many occasions had to face the wrath of the Church and the 'holier than thou' brigade."

"When you were so badly injured Icarus, you had not fallen over the cliffs as everybody told you. At that time, you had a lovely girlfriend called Daisy Maisie. She was lovely just as the pretty flower she was named after, and you adored each other. I didn't know you back then, but I am told that you were like two skylarks, singing wildly together in a bright blue summer's sky."

"Some people with dark thoughts reckoned you were seeing too much of each other, and that you should be separated before lust got the better of you. Apparently, you were both caught doing the 'dirty deed' as they called it, and they thrashed you within an inch of your life. Can you remember anything at all about that time Icarus?"

Icarus stared into the yonder and after a long time he spoke. His eyes reddened and filled with tears: "I can begin to see it now. The confusing haze is clearing. The utter frustration that had me so lost for all of those years is lifting. I begin to see it; I can taste the blood in my mouth and feel the terrible pain of that beating all over my body."

"But what joy, I can also taste the sweetness of my beautiful Daisy Maisie as she kissed me with so much love. I remember, how we were naked together as I love to be, and we held each other so close that our bodies became one. It was the most wonderful feeling of love that we shared and we shivered in ecstasy together. She was perfect: our love was perfect."

Eva spoke, "You made love then... the physical act of lovemaking? I thought that they all lied."

"If that is what it's called, then yes, we did, and as often as we could. My floppy bit grew like a prize marrow when we were close, and we went at it like rabbits."

Eva laughed fit to bursting, "Well that's what sex is, I guess you knew all the time, all apart from what it was called. Your mind shut out the memories to protect yourself, and they have remained locked-up tight until you were strong enough to cope with the truth."

Icarus remained silent as he stared into the open turf fire and eventually spoke: "You know I thought that Daisy Maisie was just a beautiful dream... someone I visited in my depths of despair, a smile that warmed me in the cold dark night, and a hand that took mine when I was lost in my nightmares. Could it be true Eva? She was far too beautiful to be real in this all too often ugly world... How can I find her? I must find her... the love of my life... my very soul."

With trepidation Eva told him of the tragic end of Daisy Maisie, and she became alarmed when she could see that he was beginning to shut down and withdraw into the dark place that had imprisoned him for so long. She rushed over to him and squeezed him as hard as she could. She kissed both of his cheeks and stared urgently into his distraught eyes as they flooded with tears.

"So, they did all of that to us because we loved too much... too fiercely? What kind of sickness is that? What topsy-turvy world do we live in that destroys love and beauty so eagerly in the name of morality? We were young and innocent, and no one told us anything. Were we evil, as I heard them shout as they battered me? Our ignorance came about by the neglect of our elders because they were too embarrassed to explain to us what is only natural? Did we deserve what they did to us?"

"Before I turn in for the night Eva, I'd like to thank you from the bottom of my heart. I love you as a true friend, but what can I say? My love for Daisy Maisie, who is lost to me forever, will always dictate that my life will never be as it should have been. A cold suffocating shadow will always be cast over me, even on the sunniest of days. Some things can never be replaced: some wounds can never heal."

Eva clasped his hand kindly with both of hers and spoke gently. "Listen to me Icarus; hold her memory in your heart like a beacon of light. Let her be your life's inspiration. Most people never know a love like you have known. An old poet called Alfie

Lord Tennis-player – I think that was his name – wrote: 'It is far better to have loved and lost than to have never loved at all.' Oh Icarus... come here laddie."

She grabbed him and tried to kiss him on his forehead but being unable to reach he swooped her up and gave her a huge smacker on the lips. "Thank you," he said, "thank you so very, very much."

Both Icarus and Eva embraced each other in the flickering light of the turf fire, neither of them wanting to let go. "Do you know that fire has never gone out for over three hundred years Icarus? Dolores proudly told me so. A turf fire has been burning continuously in their hearth since her great, great, great, great and God knows how many great grandfathers built the place. Through storms and famines and wars and disease, they kept the fire burning, even if it was only smouldering at times. However dark things became, the warmth of their home was incredibly important to them; not just the heat, but by being the comfort and friendship of their family home. It became a symbol of security and love, and they nurtured it and refused to let it die."

"Make a pact with me Icarus, keep a fire burning in your heart just the same. Continue on your life's journey, and from time to time if you need to, climb your favourite cliffs, and with the poetry that lives in your soul and the honesty that is your heart, call out as loud as you can: feck the feckin' lot of them!" They both began to laugh, and their tears of sadness became tears of joy. The both grabbed a blanket each that had been put out for them and curled up on the two cosy chairs by the fire.

Neither of them slept much and the morning crept up on them like an unexpected debt collector. Eva knew that Icarus must leave, and she wondered if she would ever see him again. She knew that history proved that the lives of individuals like Icarus often ended in tragedy. It comforted her however, that those who got to know him, really loved and adored him. She would miss him terribly of course, for her short time with him had been full of colour as opposed to her often grey and sometimes difficult life.

"It's time!" said Suzie as she brought them both a nice cup of tea. "The hearse is already outside, and the driver is waiting. Old Doug Down said that the driver thinks he is picking up some flowers for the bereaved family, and he hasn't a clue about Icarus. He wants to keep it that way because the driver is a very nervous individual. Apparently, they made him smuggle a coffin-load of Polish vodka down from the north last month, and they had to give him a week off due to his nerves and his hysterical bowel movements."

Icarus slurped his tea, "I know all about that," he grinned. "Look, I said that if I'm going to embark on such adventures, I'm going to have some fun. If I'm to be lying in some big box, it'll be as Icarus O'Toole, in full costume, naked as usual, arse feather and all. The coffin will become a large O'Toole box but without the spanners."

Eva snatched the tea from Icarus. "Can't have too much fluids, and only half a slice of toast, and make sure you go to the toilet for a good dump before you set off. It's out of respect for Mr Barrage and his family."

The driver paced impatiently about outside sucking hard on the last millimetre of his cigarette wondering what the feck the delay was, when Dolores called him into the shop for a cup of tea. "Flowers not quite ready," she explained, "just picking off a few faded petals and spraying for greenfly."

"Oh, I'm grand," said the driver eager to be on the road, "no thanks."

"The bollix is leaning on the hearse and staring at his watch," observed Dolores, "how on earth are we going to get Icarus into the box?"

"Leave it up to me," said Eva. "I'll distract him and you get Icarus installed." Eva guessed correctly that a man who suffered so much with his nerves, might be in need of a little something that would calm him down. She found him by the hearse lighting up his tenth cigarette that morning by the look of the stubs by his feet.

"Feckin' hate these long trips," he complained. "I never signed up for them. Just the funeral parlour, church and cemetery run, is what we agreed on. Just a glorified gofer, that's what I am. Taxi driver when they want to come back from the pub at three in the morning, and general dogsbody. I'm thinking of telling them to stuff their jobs up their gicker-cracks!"

"Woah," said Eva in her most calming of tones, and she lit up a joint of the finest weed money could buy. "Have a pull on this," she smiled, "I shouldn't, I know, but I give this to those in my care who are a bit wound up. It's illegal of course – but hey, it does the job! It's like a huge feather bed for the arthritic temperament."

"Dogs bollocks!" he grinned and reached out for a drag.

"Around the corner," insisted Eva, "the Gardaí are out and about early round here."

Suzie and Delores whisked Icarus outside to the hearse, climbed in the back and unscrewed the coffin lid. "Quickly!" they hissed, "Before he catches on."

Icarus, naked and in full flying-man attire, lowered himself face down into the coffin onto his bent knees. Buttocks prominent in the air he asked them to insert his arse feather as he was unable to reach round himself. "That's disgusting," complained Delores.

"But it's only my art, nothing to get worked up about," he replied meekly in his defence.

"I'll do it," snapped Suzie, "before we all get caught; but why the feck are you lying face down – surely that's very uncomfortable?"

"Oh, I'll be o.k., it's if I get caught; the first thing they'll see is my bare arse... It's a declaration; a sod off; a two-fingered gesture most artistically delivered... and I'll get a good fart in, if I am able!"

Feather proudly in position, the coffin lid was screwed down just in time as the grinning driver sauntered round to take the wheel. "Flowers are in the back," smiled Delores nervously, "and don't forget, your first port of call is Murph's garage at Larne docks. The hearse will be filthy after driving for hours. Mr Down insists on it being valeted and sparkling for Mr Barrage's family."

"Cool as a pool," he smiled, not a care in the world, and he set off north like a sailing ship in a favourable breeze, completely oblivious as to his charge. In his rear-view mirror he could see the three girls waving wildly goodbye. "That's nice," he sighed, "and I hardly know them."

As he approached the first corner that led on to the road to the motorway, an old Morris Minor pulled out behind him. It was driven by a determined little man in a grubby raincoat and a trilby pulled down over his eyes.

The drive to Larne was painfully long but without incident until the hearse approached Murph's garage. Icarus who had been struggling with cramp for the last hour, let out a mighty moan as his calves locked in agony. Icarus tried to shift his position to get some relief but only succeeded in banging the coffin lid loudly.

"What the feck's that?" shouted the driver with alarm. "Sounds like my drive-belts have gone." He immediately pulled onto the grass verge and stopped the engine. "Jaysus!" he exclaimed as the banging and moaning continued. "It's a good job I'm close to the garage or I'd be up shit creek without a paddle."

Joe Murphy who had been told to look out for the hearse had spotted him and was striding purposefully towards them. Curiosity got the better of the driver as the thumping continued, seemingly from inside the coffin space and he climbed inside before he could be stopped from discovering his stowaway. "Oh shite, it's coming from inside," he whimpered. "Hang on a minute, what have those sleeveens got me smuggling now? The gobshites; it's not their arses on the line if I get caught."

Before Joe could stop him, he had unscrewed the lid and tugged at it like a dentist pulls a tooth quickly so you don't notice what's coming. He took a frantic glance at Icarus's bare buttocks complete with arse feather, and he let out an almighty shriek. He crashed his head in panic on the inside of the roof and fell back dazed. Half-conscious he cursed, "They've conned me into smuggling again. This time it's turkeys and without a licence or livestock passports – the dirty rotten hooligans! And what the hell have they been feeding those turkeys on? That one on top farted like a bazooka and blasted out all of its tail feathers – phew it smells as if it's eaten a field full of cabbages!"

He sat down on the front bumper of the hearse, trembling like a leaf and lit up the remainder of the joint that Eva had given him for later. He took a deep pull and bent over staring at the ground between his highly polished black shoes.

The driver, who had been named Nelson by his father, after the great Brazilian F1 racing car driver Nelson Piquet, hated his name. His father had been an F1 fanatic, and he hoped to realise his unfulfilled dreams of being a racing car driver through his son. He pushed him with all of his might, through go-cart trials and all of the usual avenues that aspiring racers have to pursue. He completely ignored the obvious fact that his son's heart was just not in it.

The plain fact was that his son was terrified of speed and didn't particularly like cars or enjoy driving. His father was terribly disappointed in his weakling son. Filled with anger he was determined to punish him in some perverse way and have him somehow behind a wheel; so he forced him to take a job as a driver at the funeral parlour – or leave home. Jobs were very hard to come by in any walk of life, as were houses with their extortionate rents, so he resigned himself to his dull and ill-fitting career.

"Cheer up young fella," shouted Joe Murphy. "Go inside and my wife will make you a nice cup of tea while I get this hearse valeted and shining like snot on a brick wall."

"Feckin' turkeys this time, I can't believe they conned me into transporting feckin' turkeys. One of them, even though it was plucked, was still alive poor thing. I'd break its neck if I were you, and put it out of its misery." Nelson tottered off muttering that he was going to pack it all in when he got home, but suddenly had to sprint for the loo when his nervous bowels sought supplication.

"Strange young garsún," observed Joe as he drove the hearse into the garage. "You alright back there?"

Icarus groaned and made several attempts to kick off the coffin lid. "I will be when I get out of here and have a good stretch."

"Careful with that lid," chided Joe. "Did those three girls that sent you, not tell you what you were getting into?"

"Those three are a right pair! All I thought I was getting into was a coffin, not some kind of smuggling operation," he complained.

"Quid pro quo!" declared Joe. "You get smuggled to the ferry, and that naive Nelson garsún smuggles back a tax-free consignment of Polish vodka. Mr Barrage is our code name for the operation. Simple as a pimple!"

"Anyway quick, before you're spotted; we have to valet this vehicle and send Nelson to pick up Mr Barrage and get you on the midday ferry, all in half an hour."

Icarus, climbed out of the coffin and hastily donned his corduroy suit. A light tap on the windscreen, and an insincere cough made them look up in alarm.

"What's all this?" said Nelson who had come back for his sunglasses. "And how did you get rid of the turkeys so quickly?"

"Must be that weed you're smoking... it has you seeing things," said Joe guiltily.

"And who's this tall weird-looking fella; your new valeteer?"

"Feck off now, and don't be asking questions," snapped Joe.

"Well you hooligans," declared Nelson, "I've had enough of being used as a donkey, or is it a mule... or maybe an ass... I don't feckin' know. Anyway, the police are on their way, and I'm feckin' off."

"Oh, you gobshite," bellowed Joe. "Hold on to your trousers!" He then jumped frantically into the driver's seat with Icarus still in the coffin space at the back, did a donut, then a 'u' turn and sped off to collect Mr Barrage before the police caught up with them. Icarus was bumped and bounced about as they sped through the side streets, and after dodging frantic mothers with their prams and little yelping dogs, they miraculously arrived relatively unscathed. Nelson's father would have been impressed.

"Load her up," he screeched, "Icarus here must catch the midday ferry to Stranraer, before we head back home. That Judas Nelson has dobbed us in and they'll be looking for us on the road south with road-blocks and all."

Four men and a cheery little girl loaded up the coffin with remarkable and well-practiced skill, and in less than three minutes they were on their way again. Luckily, there were two other funeral corteges booked on the ferry that day, and they were able to slot in amongst them unnoticed on the road to the port.

At precisely twelve o'clock, the ferry to Stranraer set sail towards a new chapter in Icarus's life. Back at Murph's garage, two policemen with their highly-strung guard dog were looking up and down at Nelson. "Can you smell anything officer?" said one to the other as he sniffed at him with suspicion from an impudently close range.

Nervous Nelson

SCALING NEW HEIGHTS

VA'S SISTER WAS WAITING for him as he disembarked. She warmly introduced herself and her two young daughters who stared up at him open mouthed. "The twins," she declared, "Molly and Holly," and they grabbed on to their mammy's skirt and hid behind her legs whilst their heads popped out with irresistible curiosity. She made a grab for his scruffy little suitcase just as Eva had and asked in a sympathetic tone, "Is that all you have?"

"It's all I have in the world," he explained, "I like to travel light, but please I can manage."

Eva's sister's name was Tossa. She was the exact opposite to her, being tall and quiet and very elegant. She explained to Icarus that her name was Greek, meaning 'gift from God', and that their mother had been a sarcastic drunk who had enjoyed that her daughters were teased at school. She liked her name however, which she pronounced as Toassa, not Tossa. Tossa Caber, she explained had ceased being funny a very long time ago, and besides her married name was Macleod and that put an end to it.

After a long bus journey to Tarwathie, and a twenty-minute walk, they arrived safely at her idyllic rose covered cottage which brought back lovely memories of his own home and of times that were far less manic. Tossa and the twins wrestled over his suitcase and the twins won. Breathless, they both clung on to the handle as they showed him up to his bedroom, which he was absolutely delighted with. It was very pretty with floral curtains and tie-backs, with a beautiful patchwork quilt spread over a very large sumptuous bed.

"Eva explained that you were very tall, so my husband borrowed this from the local hotel. They have loads of American guests, and some of them are huge; apparently some of their basketball players are even as tall as you. Must be uncomfortable though flying over the Atlantic in those tiny aeroplane seats with such enormous arses! Anyway, make yourself comfortable and come down when you're ready. Supper will be at seven when my husband gets home."

Icarus had a little insecure moment, wondering if people thought he had a big arse. He smiled to himself however, remembering Salty Fraser from Slack-water House, who was tattooed all over his body from his years in the Merchant Navy. He had a spear tattooed on his left buttock, but he regretted it soon after it was done for he couldn't see the point.

Seven o'clock came but Icarus did not appear. He had fallen into a deep and well needed sleep, and his extravagant and symphonic snores had the three girls giggling. The table was laid and all was ready, so Molly and Holly were sent upstairs to knock gently on his bedroom door, which they did excitedly. The door that had not been shut properly, creaked open and the girls nervously glanced into the room. Icarus was curled up on the bed, fast asleep cuddling tightly Daisy his little dolly. The twins were delighted with their new houseguest.

Icarus opened one eye, "Oh, oh come in," he said drowsily.

"Din-dins on the table," they said in unison in the sweetest of Scottish tones.

"Be right down," he murmured as he hid his dolly under the pillow.

Tossa was bringing a bowl of steaming potatoes to the table when a knock came on the back door. "Who could that be?" she sighed for she hated mealtimes being disturbed. "The plumber's not due 'til the morning."

She quickly put the potatoes on the table and rushed to the back door clumsily trying to open it with her oven-gloves still on. "Who is it?" she called as she fumbled with the latch. Icarus who was halfway down the stairs halted.

A bony hand came around the half-open door holding a crumpled business card which read: 'Shay Monhue, sub-editor, Irish Daily Global.' A scruffy shoe followed quickly behind which jammed the door open, and a weasel-like face wearing a cynical grin tried to force its way in.

"Just a quick word, Mrs Macleod, I'm a personal friend of Icarus O'Toole, and I believe he is staying here."

At that very moment, Tossa's husband arrived home from work, by the back door as usual because of his dirty boots. Donald Macleod was a huge powerful man and was very protective of his loved ones. He picked him up by the scruffy scruff of his neck and threw him one handed into the dustbins by the back gate.

"No one here by that name, and if you ever call here again, with or without an appointment, I'll... I'll... well you'll regret it laddie!"

Donald slammed the door behind him and removed his muddy work-boots, to the crashing of dustbin lids and muffled cursing.

"Oh Donald, you promised," sighed Tossa, "we have the twins now. Those horrible days of brawling and mayhem must remain in the past. What kind of example are you setting for Molly and Holly?"

"But, he was trying to force his way in; he could have been a mad axe murderer. I was only trying to protect my family."

Outside in the back lane, Shay Monhue, was climbing into his Morris Minor. "Result!" he smirked as he ruffled potato peelings and cabbage leaves out of his hair.

Icarus descended the rest of the stairs. "Look, I'm sorry about that, I'm amazed I was found so quickly. I'll be off in the morning, I don't want to be any trouble."

"You're going nowhere," said Donald. "I eat nasty little men like that for breakfast... or I could do... if I wanted to, but of course I don't... not any..."

He glanced guiltily at Tossa who interrupted: "Don't worry about reporters, you're in Scotland now and among friends; let's eat." The twins took a hand each and led Icarus to the table.

Supper was simply wonderful. Icarus had been welcomed in to a home full of laughter and love. Tossa of course, was an excellent cook, and when she was satisfied that everyone had eaten their fill, she cleared the table with the help of the twins, then took them up to bed. Donald offered to help but Tossa insisted that he stay with Icarus and have some 'man to man' time.

"My sister-in-law tells me that you've had an unusual life to date. Don't worry Icarus, were not here to judge, I myself had a past I'm not exactly proud of. I met Eva and her sister, now my lovely wife at the Braemar Highland Games. I was Scotland's best at tossing the caber, and overall games champion for three consecutive years. Anyway, I met them in the beer-tent after I'd been awarded the gold cup, and when they told me their names, we all fell about laughing."

"They had been brought up in a tough area of Glasgow, but spent their summer holidays in their father's family home in Tarwathie – which is where we live now. They were so much fun, I didn't know who I fell for more, the little hilarious one or the tall shy one."

"Angus McBreen, who had come second to me for the third year running, and was full of whiskey, came over and started mouthing off, something about my caber being a lot lighter than his and winking to his mates – if they knew what he meant. When he offered to show the sisters his hairy caber from under his kilt, I saw red. In those days I had a very short fuse so I gave him a Glasgow kiss and he teetered backwards and crash-dived into the judges' table who were nonchalantly slurping their afternoon tea. Now Angus was a very hard man, but not very bright, which is why I always had the edge on him. He flew at me like a wild William Wallace, and I charged at him like a raging Rob Roy. We kicked seven-bells out of each other and wrecked the beer-tent and destroyed most of the flower and home-produce displays. To my shame, I really enjoyed it, but I was daft in those days."

Donald Macleod

"Her Majesty the Queen had only just left, or I am sure we would have spent ten years in Low Moss prison in Glasgow, instead of the six months we did serve. Coincidentally Eva came to visit me as my social worker and she showed me the error of my ways. I had been a scrapper most of my youth, always with the excuse that I was standing up to some bully or other – mind you Eva had been just as bad as me by all accounts, but after counselling me for those six months she persuaded me to think before I acted, which I did, but then I still kicked arseholes up the arse if they needed it."

"Upon release, Eva and I became great friends, and we and her sister would often meet up in the summer holidays. I had been banned from competing in the Highland games so I spent my days in gentler pastimes. Tossa and I became very close and we fell in love and married the next summer. Eva married herself soon after, some arrogant bollix, who had flattered her whilst going through her bank account. It didn't last and she has been alone ever since. She's a fantastic lassie with a heart as big as a planet, and we'd do anything to help her which is why you are here. You came highly recommended."

Icarus thanked Donald for sharing his past with him and observed, "We all of us have a past, but I suppose the secret is to have a future. My trouble is that I don't really care about tomorrow. I lost the love of my life..."

Donald interjected, "Ah, Daisy Maisie; Eva told us, we are all so very sorry."

Icarus continued: "Since I was injured when I was a boy, a lot of my fantasy dream world blends in to my everyday life. I sometimes can't tell what is real and what is not. Sometimes I sit on the toilet in the morning and do not know what will flush away when I pull the chain: what is in the toilet or what's squatting on it."

"I try to laugh and be as crazy as I can, because it is the only thing that makes sense to me. I can lose myself in my ridiculous art and daftness – and the pain eases. I thought I was getting better at Slack-water House, but then I was surrounded by people just like me, I belonged and felt safe. And now, even with Eva's help I am lost, and I only go on so that I don't hurt her."

Donald slowly and meaningfully stood up. He was a mountain of a man; six-feet-five and twenty-two stone of Highland-granite. He wore a magnificent black beard and spoke in a gravelly but gentle manner. "I'm away to bed now Icarus – but think on this: you've only been here five minutes and the twins adore you; my wife is moved to tears when she talks about you, and Eva tells me that is the story with everyone you meet. I personally think you're a bollix, but you can't win 'em all... no only joking Icarus; I'm very happy to have you here as a friend... so goodnight and we'll see you in the morrow."

Icarus had a warm glow inside and smiled at Donald's honesty and directness. He followed him up the stairs shortly after and cosied up into the deliciously comfy bed provided lovingly for him. He couldn't remember when he had ever slept in a bed big enough, not since he was a toddler. He stretched out and yawned, pulled his doll from under his pillow and kissed it, and immediately fell into the arms of Morpheus.

"Morning Icarus," said Donald as he placed a welcome cup of tea on his bedside table. "Any plans for today?"

"Well Eva told me about Mormond Hill that she said I should take a look at. Apparently, it is inlaid with a stag and a horse in a most beautiful way. Sounds like a kind of art I would be interested in, but it's too far to walk, perhaps there's a bus?"

Donald told him that his girls would sort him out and that he had to get to work on the farm. "What's the time?" asked Icarus looking out at the rosy sunrise.

"A quarter to six," replied Donald, "you've missed the best part of the day."

Icarus came down after his ablutions into the kitchen where the twins sat beaming at him from the far side of the table. "Pancakes today," they smiled as they shaped their hands as in prayer and clapped with delight. "Our favourite!"

"Donald tells me that you'd like to see Mormond Hill," said Tossa, "it's too far to walk, but you could borrow Eva's old bike. You'll have to raise the saddle but it should do. It's in the shed by the bins, and there's a set of spanners in the toolbox. I have to take the girls to school now and go shopping later, but I've made you a packed lunch – cheese and tomato sandwiches okay? – with a flask of tea. If you set off after breakfast, you should have plenty of time and we'll see you for supper."

Icarus could see why their mother's pancakes were their favourite, and after devouring them with childish enthusiasm and completely draining the maple syrup bottle, he put the packed lunch and his Icarus outfit into his small knapsack. Not to waste any time he went directly to the shed to inspect Eva's bike, and rummaged about for the spanners to lift the saddle. Not one of the spanners would fit the nut on the saddle, so he strained away with a pair of pliers which kept slipping off and skinning his knuckles.

"That'll have to do," he puffed in frustration, "I just hope it holds!" and even after he had raised it to its maximum height it was still ridiculously too low for him. He mounted it and managed to pedal about, but he looked like he was on a trick circus bike, designed to look impossible to ride.

His first few yards had his knees smacking him painfully under his chin, so he changed his style and pedalled with his legs wide apart. He had to pedal madly however, to maintain horizontal momentum or he stalled and fell off. It took him at least ten attempts to get going and with grazed elbows and knees, he set off optimistically, not entirely sure of his route.

He laughed his socks off as he pumped his legs up and down like pistons past his ears and then hollered out with glee: "A great Scot Called Robert Louis Stevenson once said: 'It is better to travel hopefully than to arrive,' and as we are in Scotland..."

Icarus was always up for a challenge, especially a silly one, and this was to be no exception. Each time he turned left or right, his nearside knee caught him a sharp smack under his chin, and when he sped off downhill on a twisty side-road towards Fraserburgh, his chin took a battering like a boxer's punch-bag.

Every hundred yards or so he was blinded by a bright flash, which he thought strange as there was no accompanying thunder, and just when he thought that his ride couldn't get more insane, his saddle suddenly collapsed and sprung off. He jolted downwards and impaled his arsehole painfully on the short tube that the saddle sat in, and unable to free himself, with legs flailing like a windmill, he completely lost control of his mount. Another blinding flash had him wobbling and weaving from side to side as he squealed like a stuck pig.

Inevitably disaster struck, and he crashed, flying through a hawthorn hedge and he landed upside down in a large patch of stinging nettles with the bike still firmly jammed between his buttocks. A recently familiar face pushed its way through the hawthorn and laughing out loud asked if he was alright. It was Shay Monhue, who had followed him all the way. "Jaysus, that's the funniest thing I've seen in years! Let me give you a hand."

"Feck off you gobshite," groaned Icarus as Shay gave him a rapturous round of applause.

"No, seriously," he replied, "I'd like to help. I'm not the man you think I am. (Another blinding flash had Icarus seeing stars.) Oh, let me introduce you to Mr Carlo Ratzi; my photographer. Because he has so many children – twelve in all, we call him by his nickname – Pappa."

"It's a pleasure Signore Icarus, but do you need an assistants to pull *bicicletta* from *parte inferiore*?"

The reporter and photographer climbed through the hedge and Papa held Icarus tight as Shay tugged hard on the bike. "Not what I normally do of a Tuesday," he sniggered.

Icarus was helped into the back seat of Shay Monhue's Morris Minor and he sat down very, very gingerly. It was a convertible and being a fine day, the hood was down, which was ideal for him as he could sit comfortably without hitting his head on the roof. The other two sat in the front seat and stared up at him. "You wouldn't have any cream for a sore arse?" pleaded Icarus, "I know old boys like you have trouble with dangleberries, and you might have some in your washbags."

"I think I have somathing," responded Pappa sympathetically, and he dived into his travelling bag and fumbled about until he pulled out a tube of something which he thought would do the job. The description and instructions on the tube were all in

Italian, but Icarus was so sore down below he was willing to try anything.

"I can't see to put it on properly," protested Icarus as he unscrewed the cap, "one of you will have to do it."

The three of them were a good ten miles down the road before anyone spoke. "If you breathe a word, Pappa, about the ointment, you'll be needing it yourself after pulling your camera out of your own arse."

Icarus, leant back in grateful relief, "No need to be embarrassed," he smiled, "just make sure that you clean your hands before you hand me one of those sandwiches."

'Pappa' Ratzi and Shay Monhue

They all burst out laughing as the car with Eva's buckled bike, headed out to Mormond Hill as they had agreed. Shay began to open up as he drove along and told Icarus about his time as a young reporter and the ambitions he once had to be a published writer. His eyes narrowed as he told him tale after tale of rejection of his writings and how he had given up disheartened many years ago.

"As an aspiring novelist I was only mediocre to be truthful," he confessed, "but I do have a bloodhound's nose for a good story. As time went by, I covered stories about the most horrendous things, and I was becoming a cynical old bastard..."

"Was?" interrupted Pappa.

"Okay, okay!" replied Shay... "As I was saying – I also wrote about the most heart-warming stories that partly restored my faith in human nature, but the darkness that I uncovered began to eat away more and more at me, and overshadowed any good that I wrote about. I only plodded on because it was my living, but each day I became increasingly disillusioned. I was suffocating."

"About a year ago I had to renew my health insurance, and the insurance company that I had my policy with, insisted that I had to have a medical in order to continue with my cover. So, I went to the Matter Hospital in Dublin where they gave me a good going over. They tapped and listened to my chest and drained an armful of blood – and you'd like this Icarus, they stuck a gloved finger up my arse and started feeling about for something or other. They took my blood pressure which of course had gone through the roof, and then sent me for a chest X-ray. I waited for nearly four hours when finally, two nurses came out muttering to each other and holding up various charts and the X-ray, and then they told me to wait for the consultant who would be along presently."

"I waited for a further two hours, and by that time it was well past midnight. I was bored, tired and hungry, so I fecked off home. I had forgotten all about it when two months later, a letter from the insurance company came stating that due to an undisclosed medical condition, they could not give me cover and were terminating my policy with immediate effect."

"Of course, I panicked and phoned the hospital. It took me ages to talk to anyone and even then, I was given some nebulous excuse and blamed everything on staff shortages. I phoned the insurance company who were reluctant to tell me anything until one day I got through to a call centre in India who let it slip in broken English that I only had two weeks left to live, and that the letter from the hospital was already three weeks old."

"I was shaken to my boots in panic. I started to think seriously about all aspects of my life, and overnight I became a changed person. I decided to concentrate on what was good and noble in my life."

"Holy Mama of Jaysus," said Pappa, "I'm not knowing this abouta you."

"Ah, it was all bollix; turns out it was only my life policy that had two weeks left. My results giving me a clean bill of health never got to me because I had fecked off. So anyhow – only myself to blame. I had a soul-searching couple of weeks, and this is me now – a sentimental even ethical old hack... but still nobody's fool."

"So, you see Icarus, I mean you no harm, and your art interests me. It's your honesty and lack of bullshit – well, perhaps not that, but your integrity that I admire. I love your sense of the ridiculous, and how you love to laugh. I know now that life is too important to be taken too seriously, and I want to write about you; I want to be along for the ride."

"I'd fix that saddle first!" added Icarus with a grin.

"Seriously though, I know about the tragedies in your life and the goings on in your neck of the woods, and I've been biding my time. There is corruption, hypocrisy, and downright wickedness to be found everywhere."

"I'll reveal it all using your personal story as the central theme. Pappa here will photograph all of your works and we'll compile it all into a book which we can serialise and syndicate in all the important newspapers. What do you think Icarus? And we could have some serious fun along the way."

Icarus, always eager for a good laugh, was keen to get started immediately. "I suppose I'll have to trust you," he said, "not to make a fool of me, and not to let me down."

"You have my promise," affirmed Shay, "so long as you don't let on about the arse-ointment."

Icarus as sharp as a razor replied: "Arse no questions, tell no lies!"

"*Mama mia!*" cheered Pappa, "*Fa un comico in questi giorni.*"✳

Soon after they arrived at Mormond Hill, and they all got out to have a walk around. Icarus explained that he wanted to do his art performances on the tops of such hills, to make them appear more dramatic, and Pappa agreed saying that the scenery would make great backdrops for the photographs.

For a trial run Icarus put on his outfit and went to position himself by the stag which had been laid down in white quartz rocks in eighteen-seventy to commemorate the wedding of the Laird. He decided to pose amid the antlers as Pappa set up his tripod, but he turned and minced down the hill shaking his head. "Can't do it," he complained to Shay, "my arse is too sore to take a feather… just pass that cream over would you!"

Pappa dug it out of his toilet bag once more and gave it to Shay to pass over to him and whispered into his ear. "Don't a tell; it's a called Wonder-white toothpaste… placebo affect… he'll have the whitest arse-hole in a Scottyland – and it will no have a bad-breath!"

It was late afternoon, and they decided to turn around and head back to Tarwathie. Shay suggested that perhaps it would be wise not to mention their meeting as yet. "That Macleod man has the strength of Hercules, I don't want to piss him off again," he declared, "so we'll drop you off at the end of the lane, if that's okay."

"I suggest you think about your performances and where you'd like them to take place – and take some time out. Enjoy your stay with the Macleods, they are good people, and call me when you want to begin. We're having a break too. Pappa here wants to

✳   Italian: everyone's a comedian these days.

capture the Loch Ness monster on film, and I want to capture a monster of my own in the shape of the salmon I promised myself if I ever found the time to take up fishing. We'll be staying at the Loch Ness Lodge at Drumnadrochit... here's the number."

Icarus tucked into his back pocket the scrap of paper with the number on it, and lifted Eva's saddleless and battered bike out of the boot. He waved his two new friends goodbye, and with delicate steps he slowly made his way up the lane to the Macleods' cottage.

"You okay?" shouted Donald as he watched Icarus struggle with Eva's bike as he came into the back yard. "I'll give you a hand," and he put down the basket of washing that he had been hanging on the line and went to his assistance.

"Came off the bike," he groaned.

"I'm not surprised," laughed Donald. "I meant for you to take my bike, not Eva's. Tossa couldn't have heard me properly when I shouted from the shed this morning... ah well, come inside laddie, this calls for a wee dram."

Icarus in all of his years had never tasted alcohol. Something in his distant memory – perhaps tales about his father's drinking had always put him off. He had refused a swig of the illicit Polish vodka before catching the ferry, much to the indignance of Joe Murphy, but as his arse was throbbing like a short-sighted stonemason's thumb, he thought it might take his mind off it.

Donald's wee dram was a generous 'Highland hospitality' measure. He declared to Icarus that two fingers was the accepted measure, but with hands like coal shovels, he almost filled the glass. He asked Icarus about Mormond Hill and he listened with interest:

"You know here in Scotland, we have a series of mountains called Munros; there are two hundred and eighty-two of them and they are all stunning. Why don't you choose the ones that interest you and we could all do a reconnoitre? I have a book upstairs, with them all in, but my personal favourite is Slioch by bonnie Loch Maree in the Highlands. It towers over three-thousand, two-hundred and twenty-feet high, and is absolutely majestic."

Icarus squirmed on his seat but listened intently to Donald. "I have an idea to pose as Rodin's great sculpture 'The Thinker'. It could be a perfect setting, high on a mountain, like a great philosopher, but what does Slioch mean in English?"

"It translates as spear, as in the pointed weapon, the word being of Greek origins and then taken into Gaelic."

Icarus smiled from ear to ear, fascinated by Slioch's etymological past. "Imagine," he smiled to himself, "what Salty Fraser would say if he knew that I was about to have a three-thousand feet tall spear under my bare arse!"

Tossa and the twins poked their heads around the kitchen-door and called their boys in for supper. Icarus took his seat opposite them, and the girls did their normal grinning act. They then ran around to him and plonked a large sheet of paper on his lap. "They've done a drawing of you at school," said Tossa, "and they'd like to give it to you."

"Oh, that's marvellous," replied Icarus as he turned it left and right to find which way up it was. It had been done in bright coloured felt-tipped pens, and it had toilet rolls and tissue paper and buttons and all manner of things glued to it, followed by a liberal shaking of glitter and a handful of dried pasta.

"May I keep it?" he asked gently as if it was the most precious thing in the world.

"If you like it," said the girls in unison.

"Like it...? I love it!" he said with genuine emotion, and yet again the twins were delighted, as were their parents who glanced at each other in contentment.

Throughout supper, Icarus continued to squirm on his seat, hoping that he would not be noticed. The meal was as tasty as tasty could be, and the twins had them highly amused with their account of their day at school. Tossa, in trying to maintain good table manners chided them for talking too much during meal times, and they all nearly fell off their chairs laughing when she told them not to talk with their mouths open.

When supper was over their daddy gave them a little nod in the direction of the stairs, and they rushed over to him and gave him a big kiss and a hug, and then danced over to Icarus and gave him the very same. Tossa swooped them up in her arms and gave them both a huge hug then climbed the wooden hills with them as she put it.

"Another wee dram?" asked Donald.

"I suppose so," replied Icarus as he shuffled his backside from side to side in search of relief.

Tossa came back down the stairs with a smile on her face and Donald barked out of the blue: "He's got a sore bum!"

Icarus thought it impossible for him to be embarrassed, but on this occasion, he blushed ever so slightly.

"Don't be embarrassed," said Tossa, "Donald often had it when he first got his bike, you were often saddle-sore weren't you darling?"

"Sure was, but four hours sitting on a bucket of cracked ice did the job."

"Oh, don't tease him Donald," tutted Tossa, "go and bring down that calamine lotion from the bathroom cabinet."

Tossa smiled sweetly at Icarus, "I've good news, Eva is coming to stay with us at the weekend. The twins will be excited, so we must have a barbecue if the weather is fine. It would be nice to introduce you to our friends."

Donald came down the stairs shaking the bottle vigorously.

"Are you sure about this Tossa, I took two teaspoons four times a day for a week, and it did nothing for me – honestly, I might as well have shoved it up my arse!"

"Och, away with you, Donald! Don't torment the man," and unable to stop herself from laughing, she bent over holding on to her middle and let out a mighty guffaw.

Donald handed the bottle to Icarus and apologised. "Don't mind me," he smiled, "we just enjoy pulling each other's legs in this house. Did I hear you say that Eva is coming this weekend Tossa?"

"Yes, that's right Donald, she'll be arriving on the four o'clock bus to Fraserburgh. Luckily, Duncan McPhew has some bits and pieces to pick up at the ironmongers, so he said he'll bring her the rest of the way."

Donald gave a wry smile. "I hope he doesn't do his normal trick of coming back cross-country. He uses old farm tracks and cuts across fields, so he can enjoy the fresh air and avoid the car fumes."

"He can't be serious," laughed Tossa, "that old diesel tractor of his hasn't been serviced in years – have you seen the black smoke that billows out of the back? Anyway, I can't fetch her, the girls have pibroch* practice at four. She'll have to manage, and I know she'll enjoy the scenery."

Donald said good night and excused himself, explaining that he was doing relief milking at four in the morning. Tossa poured a small whiskey for herself after Icarus had refused one, and she bade him to join her next door in front of the fire.

She eased herself into her comfy chair and kicked off her shoes. She stretched out her legs and lowered her feet onto a beautifully embroidered footstool.

"My mother made that," she said with pride, "in fact it's the only thing that Eva and I have of hers. We only knew her as a bitter old woman, and although our lovely dad always made excuses for her, she was very hard work."

"Dad used to tell us of how she was as a young woman, before she took to the drink. She was very artistic and bright and breezy as a summer's day. She'd spend hours doing watercolours of the wild flowers in the meadows behind her house from being a very small child."

"She loved nature and all beautiful things, and was wonderful with her hands. She wanted to go to art-school when she was old enough, but her parents were poor, and she had to take a job at the local bakery. That suited her down to the ground though, as the very early shifts often starting at half four and finishing at noon, meant that she had the rest of the day to be creative."

"When she was eighteen, she met my father who was just like her in many ways. They fell in love and married quite quickly and soon after Eva came along and unexpectedly about four years later, I joined them which made our family complete. There was

---

* Scottish Gaelic: the tartan hoover; instrument favoured for 'Scotland the Brave'.

no malice in the naming of us because Eva was Christened Eve, and my name, as you know is not meant to be pronounced as tosser. All that stupidity came much later, inspired by her mood swings and fuelled by the drink."

"And it wasn't the drink, Icarus that ruined her, that was just an effect of her broken spirit. It was the frustration she suffered from being rejected and neglected as an artist, which is why I am telling you about her. For years she would send her beautiful paintings and other works of art, including the most wonderful small bronze sculptures, to the various academies about the world. She was always turned down: not once did she have a piece of art shown at any of the academy summer exhibitions, anywhere."

"One day, dad found her in tears over another rejection letter, and they both agreed to visit the exhibition to see what was being accepted. Later that August they went, and dad found her staring open mouthed at a large watercolour entitled 'The Origins of Harmonic Disharmony'. Dad said that it was an old cereal packet squashed flat with three smudged rings of colour applied from a plastic paint bottle. The catalogue lauded it as a work of great humanity and integrity, and it had two pages of gobbledegook underlining its brilliance."

"Our mother – Fenella was her name, shook in anger and started pulling at her hair and screaming. She didn't say a word for the whole journey home and for the following month she never got out of bed – I remember well taking meals up to her on a tray with Eva, when we were very small, and taking them back down again untouched."

"The doctor came and prescribed tablets for depression, and she just turned into some kind of zombie. When she started drinking, she started to turn nasty, and when we hid the bottles and eventually emptied the house of any booze, she would go down to the local shops and steal it. Dad often had to try to defend her in court in front of unsympathetic judges, and one even tried to suggest they were in it together. It was not an easy time for any of us."

"But dad refused to abandon her. He remembered her bright self and ignored all of the abuse, yet we as children began to hate her. When she died of a combination of painkillers and three bottles of whiskey, I to my shame was glad, Eva refused to speak of her, but dad was devastated."

"My point to you Icarus is this: during her illness – which I now consider it to have been, she took on a pseudonym and sent in artwork as before. She painted still-lifes blindfolded using an old toothbrush and old hair-dye, and she had more success. She even won a silver medal one year. That is what sealed her fate. That is what destroyed her soul, and before she died, she burned every piece of art that she had ever created, all but this footstool which she had given to dad for his birthday"

"Tread carefully Icarus because my mother was driven nuts by her art. Would I be correct in saying that you started off as nuts, and that your art is steering you to sanity? And think on Icarus, you may become well known and eventually admired by many, but the artworld can be fickle and cruel in the extreme. My mother's art and yours are like chalk and cheese, yet I feel she would have understood your intent and admired your sincerity."

"Do not be like my mother who allowed her art to break her heart. Her struggle came about because she truly believed that art and beauty were exactly the same thing, and that they could not and should not be separated. She insisted that 'in the eye of the beholder', referred only to personal taste, and that beauty was a fundamental truth; a pinnacle of excellence and perfection within itself, which we all in some way should strive for. An artist's role for her was to demonstrate this to the world, that beauty lay all around us and it should be nurtured and cherished. As she became more depressed and more disillusioned, she would grunt to herself: 'Swine... I'm casting pearls before swine!' which was ironic, because owing to the decline of her self-worth, she began to behave and live like a pig herself."

Icarus did not speak for a while and the room remained silent apart from the comforting crackle of the logs on the fire. "I'm not really an artist like your mother," he eventually confessed, beginning to feel a bit of a fraud, "but I do have something to say.

I find the world to be ridiculously wonderful; obscenely beautiful yet happily cruel. I want the world to see how precious every moment is because our next breath could be our last: that is what I want my art to say. My new performances are meant to take people out of their comfort zone and make them aware of their living and spiritual selves... Jaysus," he seethed, "my arse is burning like brushwood fire!"

The conversation ended abruptly as Icarus grabbed the bottle of camomile lotion and shook it wildly as he shot up the stairs like a man possessed. At four in the morning, Donald found him scrambling about in the fridge for ice having already grabbed a galvanised bucket from under the sink. Not wanting to embarrass him further, he slipped quietly out of the back door. He couldn't help but smile to himself as he knew that the only ice that was in the fridge was a solitary ice-lolly. "Should fit nicely though," he whispered to himself, "and it is a raspberry-ripple!"

At seven o'clock Tossa found him fast asleep sitting on the galvanised bucket. She didn't really want to wake him to spare him any embarrassment, but she didn't want the twins to find him in such a state. "Scuse me Icarus," she said gently as she nudged his shoulder. "The children will be down..."

Icarus sat bolt upright as if he had been clattered from behind by an angry farmer while he had been the lookout for his pals raiding his orchard.

"What the feck," he blurted out and fell over sideways with the bucket firmly jammed onto his backside.

He apologised profusely as he struggled up the stairs with the bucket clinging to him like a limpet. He fell into his bedroom backwards with a clatter, and with some difficulty managed to wriggle free. He examined his rear-view in the full-length mirror admiring the red-raw ring surrounding his buttocks and sighed with relief as the lollipop stick slipped out with a plop. Then he shook his head and looked up to the ceiling and declared: "Jaysus... what is it with me and my arse?"

By the time he came downstairs again, everyone had left, but a nice continental breakfast was waiting for him on the table, and a note from the twins with two big kisses on it. "Have a nice day," is all it said, but it made him feel wonderful.

Icarus had a lazy day. He read Donald's book about the Munros that he had left on the breakfast table for him, and lowered himself down into the easy chair in the kitchen, where Tossa had left an inflatable rubber ring for his comfort. With no one in the house and nothing particular to do, he started to think seriously about his work and what his schedule should be.

"Icarus O'Toole, the incredible naked flying man doesn't actually take off," he mused, "but these next events will really launch my career. I hope that people get it; that my flights are flights of imagination and of fantasy. My wings are only symbolic of a desire to throw off the earth-bound shackles of everyday drudgery."

"We all of us should take flight into the wonderful world of creativity; of art and music and dance. We must fill our souls to the brim with beauty and collectively save the world. Who was that Russian guy, Fyodor Dusty-Hoffski... or something ski? Anyway, he wrote a book about an idiot, and quotes: 'Beauty will save the world,' and I agree. On a lovely sunny spring morning, folk are less inclined to kick the dog."

"So, my next major performance will be as 'The Thinker', on top of Slioch. Sunday the fifth of August will give me enough time to get organised, and as it is to be a Sunday, I must get a new brightly coloured rudder-feather for my Sunday best – and of course, out of respect for the day."

"I should do a round dozen of the most spectacular Munros; one a week say, and if all that goes to plan, I should try further afield. I should do the Eifel Tower in Paris; I'll call my installation 'The Trifle Tower' and squat on a huge bowl of jelly and custard and give out free spoons for everyone to join in."

"Then there's the Empire State's building in New York, following King Kong of course, and the Petronas Twin Towers in Malaysia. I could shoot the rapids at Niagara Falls – that would be a barrel of laughs! – and not forgetting the Taj Mahal in India, which is described as 'a solitary tear on the cheek of time'. I'm exhausted just thinking about it all!"

"I must get in touch with Shay, in that case, no time to waste... he'll have things to organise, and he may have some suggestions himself. I'll also need a plinth with the title 'The Thinker', and a load of psychobabble that describes it – without of course being gobbledegook. The eminent seventeenth century French philosopher, René Dustcartes' quote '*Cogito, ergo sum*'* will fit perfectly."

Icarus was very happy with himself, and got up to make a fresh pot of tea, when the door opened with a cheery shout of "Hello, anyone at home?"

It was Eva just in from her cross-country safari on Duncan McPhew's rickety tractor. "Jaysus – a bigger bollix never put his arm through a coat! That tractor seat was hard steel and we bounced up and down on those rutted tracks like eejits. I wonder if they've still got some calamine lotion in the bathroom cabinet."

Icarus poured out a cup of tea for Eva and himself, and soon after, she descended the stairs delicately. "Oh, I see the rubber ring's out already. Someone else with a sore bum?"

Icarus explained his predicament and of course Eva burst out laughing. "Daft as it may sound Icarus, about a year ago I and the whole family were sore in the nether regions. Donald from his new bike, and I from my old bike after a non-stop cycle tour to John O'Groats up north. Tossa and the twins had been pony-trekking in unseasonably hot weather and we were all itching like mad."

"So, I phoned the local health centre and told them that we needed urgent help as we were all scratching ourselves to death as we all had sore arses. The nurse told me it was a serious condition and that we might have to be hospitalised, and that the doctor would be round immediately with an ambulance on standby."

"We all panicked apart from my lovely calm sister Tossa, who phoned them straight back and told them that we had sore arses, not psoriasis."

Again, Icarus and Eva were in fits, rolling about holding their middles when the rest of the family came home and wondered what was so funny.

---

*   Latin: I think therefore I am.

"Oh, nothing," said Eva unable to stop, "normal daft stuff," as the twins dived on her squealing with excitement.

"We're having a barbecue tomorrow, said Tossa, just to celebrate you two guys being here. Nothing fancy, and we have invited the normal suspects. Some of Donald's family have threatened to come down from the Isle of Skye, but I'll believe it when I see it."

"Have you invited Donald's dishy brother Fergus?" said Eva hopefully.

"Och, he's been invited every year, but he's always too busy, but who knows...?"

Eva danced with Donald's brother at their wedding and she never forgot it. He took her breath away as no one ever had, but they never had chance to meet again as he was tied to his farming high in the Cuillin mountains on Skye. "Why oh why did I marry the gobshite I did?" she sighed to herself in utter frustration.

Donald and the twins helped Tossa in with the shopping and then they all sat down at the table for tea and Tossa's homemade flapjacks. Icarus shared his story about the time he baked his drain-cleaner flackjacks, and about the little stall by his back-gate when he was a small boy. Again, laughter shook the house.

Eva asked her nieces if they wouldn't mind going up to their bedroom to play, as she had to talk about some very boring grown-up stuff. They flitted up the stairs like wind-blown butterflies, not really wanting to go and naughtily hovered about the landing and tried to listen in.

Eva put on her 'I'm not messing about now' voice: "Well I've good news and bad news. I'll start with the bad: I've had a compulsory purchase order slapped on my apartment. Some bullshit about radon gas being found leaking from under the foundations. I have been offered two hundred and fifty euro by Doctor Mead, which apparently I should be grateful for as the land is toxic and worthless and the whole street will probably have to be demolished."

"I have been trying to contact the laboratory commissioned to do the radon gas testing, but no one ever answers the phone. I had a letter from a journalist, called Shay Monhue, who incidentally is a big fan of yours Icarus, and he is on the case – he's been very helpful actually."

"Is that the bollix I kicked out of here the other day?" said Donald rather shamefacedly.

"Told you Donald," tutted Tossa, "Sometimes you…"

"Oh, I know, I know," apologised Donald, "please go on Eva."

"Well I was so cross that I couldn't think clearly, so I phoned Mr Monhue, and he told me about the close-knit self-serving Mafia inspired bunch of sleeveens that were responsible – and how he was working out a plan to bring them all crashing down. He explained that he had to be very careful though, as some of those concerned were in exalted positions and enjoyed the protection of those considered to be untouchables."

"Good, I said, the bigger they are the harder they fall. You know he's staying not too far from here with his Italian photographer friend. I think he said they were fly fishing for the Loch Ness monster, but I must have got that wrong. We should invite them to the barbecue; and Donald you'll have chance to apologise."

"Och, I suppose so. What's his number? I'll phone and ask him myself."

"And the good news?" asked Tossa eagerly.

"Well, I had to move out for the council workers dressed in feckin' great space-suits who began boarding up the street; so I moved in with my great friends Dolores and Suzie McWaggon. I had my mail redirected there, and feck me, the fan mail that you are getting Icarus is amazing. I've over three-hundred letters in my suitcase for you, and Dolores said a further fifty-five came in the post this morning after I left. The postman is making an official complaint and whinging to his union representative about being overloaded and treated like a pack-mule. Apparently, he is seeking compensation unless he gets for some kind of motorised trolley."

"The editor of a famous arts magazine called 'Arts Bi-annual' phoned me before I left asking about rumours of your forthcoming installations, but I couldn't tell him much cos I didn't know. He began to get very pushy, going on about the importance of his magazine, and how it would put you on the map, but he changed his tune when I asked him why his magazine targeted only bisexuals. He snapped back saying that it was published twice yearly and that he didn't like my homophobic and bigotry insinuations. I think I lost you that publicity Icarus, cos I told him to stick his magazine in the place you like to put your rudder-feather."

Eva pulled out a carrier bag from her suitcase and tipped the contents onto the table. "Jaysus," said Icarus, "I've never had a letter before in my life!"

They all helped him to go through his fan mail, and mostly they were very encouraging. Some were very funny, some quite sad, but all were welcome. Some even had money in them: 'For the cause,' or something similar was often written as an anecdote. So far in total, donations added up to a little over five hundred euro.

"We're all delighted for you," said Eva with pride. "You'll be able to finance your installations and pay for materials and transport etc."

Icarus was very pleased, but for him it was like enjoying a large ice-cream cornet with a wasp buzzing around it. Tossa's tale of her mother had unsettled him somewhat and he began to feel even more of a fraud. Tossa was very intuitive and guessed how he was feeling.

"Take heart Icarus," she said tenderly, "all people of worth doubt themselves at times. The philosopher Descartes himself said that seekers of truth must do so at some stage in their lifetime."

With that, everyone went about their own business and met for supper where the topic of conversation was the barbecue. The twins were pleased to have Eva sharing their room and they went to bed early as everyone did in order to be well rested for the next day's gathering.

Donald rose early as usual and began to prepare everything: chairs and picnic tables, napkins and all and sundry. He even painstakingly threaded gayly coloured bunting about the yard to set the atmosphere as he put it. He told everyone that it was the original celebratory bunting used at Glenfinnan to welcome

Bonnie Prince Charlie for the seventeen forty-five Jacobite rebellion. Nobody dared to contradict him.

He also loved to be in control of the barbecue, and he would not be separated from his tongs and charcoal. For him it was like being Chieftain of the Macleods, and he had a Highlander's responsibility to provide hospitality and shelter if needed.

He lit the barbecue at midday precisely, discussing with his old Highland games rival and now great friend, Angus McBreen, the merits of reducing the flames to a glowing grey ash, so as not to cremate the food. Angus and Donald had buried the hatchet, or in their case the caber years ago. "Aye we were daft in those days," they would often agree as they recalled for the umpteenth time one of their adventures.

Tossa was very proud of their friendship as she had encouraged it. She had told them that all the kicking and punching was completely unacceptable and that she would knock their heads together if they didn't stop, which had them all giggling.

As their friendship grew, she could see how they shared so much, but the stories, she told them, of the old days were starting to wear a bit thin.

"Aye!" said Angus, "It seems nostalgia is a thing of the past."

"True, true!" agreed Donald, "Nostalgia ain't what it was."

"Pass me the sausages Angus. You know they were much tastier and juicier when we were boys. Do you remember old butcher McPorker? Yes, of course you do; his daughter went out with your brother for a while until... well let's not talk about that, but he had a secret ingredient gathered from high in the heather-clad hills. No sausage today compares..."

"Oh, enough, enough," interrupted Tossa, "nostalgia is alive and well and living in Tarwathie."

Icarus came over to join them. He was starving. He had been on a long walk first thing, and the smell of the barbecue had called him home. Other guests began to drift in; there was no set-time as everything was very informal. There were neighbours and friends and family of all different shapes and sizes, but Icarus towered above them all and everyone was intrigued and eager to meet him. It was a splendid gathering, with warmth and mirth aplenty.

Leg pulling was an artform among the Macleods, and when Donald's long-awaited brother Fergus arrived, a shout rose up like a battle cry: "I see you're still incinerating defenceless sausages, Donald!"

"Well, they wouldn't be so burnt," he bellowed back, "you're only ten years late for yer scran!"

If anything, Fergus was even bigger than Donald and the two of them embraced each other like colliding continents.

"Holy caca!" gasped Pappa who had just arrived with Shay. "This is the land of giants!"

"Apart from me," giggled Eva as she hastily introduced herself and then dashed off to greet Fergus.

"Get shots of everything," urged Shay. "I've a feeling that today will be very special. A great introduction to Icarus's compendium of art."

Icarus felt wonderfully at home. It felt just like his time at Slack-water House – nice and nuts. He had a very serious conversation with Duncan McPhew and his gamekeeper Rory Finlay about the dangers of haggis hunting in the fog. "Aye," said Rory with a trembling voice, "they're very well camouflaged and you could stand over one without knowing it. It'd be up your kilt like a shot, clinging tightly to your personal shrubbery for shelter."

"It's true man," added Duncan, "never doubt it an inch, and once up there, they hang on with a grip of steel. It happened to young Douglas two years ago when he was out in the mist, high on Glencock Moor searching for his lost sheepdog."

"Och aye, Icarus," bleated Rory, as he pointed a quivering bony finger towards the hills, "it had been a terrible season for the haggis. Burns' Night was almost upon us, and we had none for the celebration. We had to get him unconscious drunk and wheel him in on a drinks trolley for the cutting of the haggis with the ceremonial sword; but it all ended up in tragedy when they insisted on pouring whiskey up his kilt and setting it all on fire."

"It's no word of a lie," continued Duncan, "young Douglas came round and chased about the place screaming, and the whole place was set on fire. The High Chieftain's seat of Mucklemish Castle took seven days to burn down and no one ever saw young Douglas again."

"Well he's over there youse bampots, serving out the drinks," mocked Eva, who'd heard it all before. "Did they invite you to go haggis stalking yet?"

"Oh, you're very welcome here Icarus," said Rory and Duncan in fits of laughter, "we normally get told to boil our heids after the first line!"

Icarus and Eva joined in, and the laughter was infectious, but then a war cry on the bagpipes pierced the hilarity like a highland claymore sword. Though very young, Holly and Molly were talented and sensitive pipers, and the mood of the gathering took a more sombre tone. Donald stood up on the stage he had built that morning from old pallets, and with a fierce purpose he stared hard at every single guest. "Dinnae worry," he bellowed like a highland stag, "there's enough ale for a week. Enough even for the Macleods over from Skye."

"Are you sure about that Donald?" shouted Angus as he downed in a few seconds a huge hunting horn which held five pints, and then turned it over his head to prove it was empty.

"Aye laddie, even for you," he declared as they all cheered like mad. "Today is very special as all gatherings are. We have family and friends old and new. We even have my brother Fergus to our wonderment – we thought he'd been taken from the Cuillin by a beansith, or as our Irish guests would call it, a banshee, and because we heard he liked wild women, we thought he was lost forever."

Eva who had been drooling over Fergus quickly transformed her doe-like countenance into the stare of an eagle. "Feck me, maybe I'm in with a shout!" she gasped, trying not to shout.

Donald continued: "But a very heartfelt welcome to you all. We have in our midst today a very special friend. An Irishman – but we'll forgive him for that – Icarus O'Toole, the famous artist who has graced us with his presence for the last few days. We the Macleods from the Cuillins of Skye, would like to honour him by presenting him with the ceremonial hunting tartan kilt. Come forward Icarus and take your place as an honorary clansman."

Icarus was astonished, and he stepped forward. Donald shook him firmly by the hand and handed him over the kilt as everyone cheered.

"Try it on," they all shouted as he respectfully examined it.

"The ceilidh is about to start, so it would be nice to see you dance in it," said Donald, "but I hope it fits; the tailors on Skye are used to big sizes, but not XXXXL!"

The music fired up all of the guests and the ale fuelled them further. Tossa, who had a beautiful voice sang a song that brought

Tossa and the Twins

them all to tears: 'Farewell to Tarwathie,' a sad song about her great great-grandfather who left to hunt the whales off the cold coast of Greenland. When she had finished people were crying into their ale, thinking about Scotland's melancholy past, when Icarus stepped into their midst wearing his tartan kilt in full splendour. It was a bit on the short side – or to be more accurate, a lot on the short side, and yet again, a huge cheer of approval roared up, and they all laughed hysterically when someone shouted: "Donald where's his trewsers?"

Icarus of course was an excellent dancer, as was Eva, and they put on a show that had them all enthralled. Each time Icarus pirouetted, Eva tried to grab the hem of his kilt to cover his under-carriage, which she mostly missed, much to the shrieking delight of the old lassies sitting close by under the stage.

He thought that he was in heaven. He knew that the Scots never wore anything under a kilt, and so he danced as if he was stamping out a forest fire. It all looked like some kind of new Scottish jive, and it caught on, everyone spinning around whilst hanging on to the hem of their partner's kilt. Shay and Pappa never had such fun, and the frenetic flash on his camera illuminated and recorded it all.

No one ever calls an end to such gatherings, they somehow just fizzle out and drift away. At four in the morning when the sun was thinking about dawn, Icarus stood among the debris and slumbering throng. He had his little scruffy suitcase packed and he smiled to himself as he looked across to the Cairngorm Mountains. Donald came up behind him quietly: he looked hurt.

"Were you going to leave without saying goodbye?" he asked.

"I'm sorry, Donald," he replied. "I lost the most important people of my life with no chance of a goodbye, and ever since, when I should be saying goodbye; I can't. Too much of my heart has been torn from me and I am afraid that I may leave behind more of my heart than I can spare. If I close myself up, like a secure strong-box, my feelings can't spill out and deplete me further."

"But what about the twins…? They won't understand; they think the world of you, as do Tossa and Eva."

Icarus was unable to explain as he didn't understand his feelings himself; it was as if he needed to punish himself for how he was. "Please say goodbye for me," he said, "and thank you for allowing me to be part of the Macleods, even if it was just for a while," And with a suffocating sadness, he slowly slipped through the back gate towards the main road. Tears reddening his eyes, he was locked rigidly facing forward, as in the grip of a vice, completely unable to turn around to smile and wave a fond farewell.

Donald however waved after him, like a highland warrior brandishing a broadsword and shouted: "What do you mean if it was just for a while? You're of the clan Macleod now, and we'll all be at Slioch in August... and that's a promise!"

Towards the Munros

THE EYE OF
THE BEHOLDER

ICARUS LOST HIMSELF IN the Highlands, but he had been in good spirits. He had hiked from glen to glen, over mountains and moorland, and had enjoyed the most magnificent scenery. What he didn't enjoy though were the frenzied squadrons of midges, especially when he rehearsed 'The Thinker' on several lesser-trod Munros. They were particularly curious about his rudder-region and he was pestered without mercy. He had been staying in bothies for all of that time and had not been into a town for weeks and so had been unable to purchase any repellent, but apart from defending his arse, all had been peaceful.

He had not eaten much over the last few days as he hadn't much food with him, but he drank and bathed in the sparkling mountain streams and he felt purified. He had time to do a lot of thinking and wondered how his life would have been with Daisy Maisie. He was unable to dwell for long on the lovelier parts of his life as it filled him with a pain which he could not reconcile, so he put such thoughts out of his mind as best he could.

He was due to do his performance of 'The Thinker' in two days' time, but his enthusiasm was on the wane, and he hadn't been in touch with anyone. Unbeknown to him, Shay Monhue had done some pre-publicity, informing those who had an interest in his demise, that the performance would be on top of Ben Nevis, Scotland's highest Munro; but everyone in the know were heading out and camping close to Slioch on the bonnie banks of Loch Maree – in their thousands.

The evening before, Icarus sat in the doorway of the bothy, and marvelled at the magnificence of the rising amber moon, when a voice behind him spoke softly. "Would you mind if I shared the bothy with you tonight? I am heading for Ullapool to catch the ferry for the Isle of Lewis, but I won't make it before dark."

Icarus turned around to see who it was, but he was obscured in the fading light.

"It would be my pleasure," he replied, with a gentleness and calmness that was growing in place of his manic self and colourful language. "Allow me to introduce myself, I am Timmy O'Toole."

"A pleasure to make your acquaintance, but if you don't mind, I am on a kind of spiritual journey, a pilgrimage if you like, and anonymity is important to me. It is meant to be a solitary journey, in isolation to concentrate the mind. I will shake your hand however."

Icarus took his gentle handshake and he caught a fleeting glimpse of him as he inched out of the shadows. He thought that he noticed a white collar as he stepped back, but he could not be sure.

"I've a big day tomorrow," he declared, "so I'll need an early night if that suits you Mister – whatever your name is."

"That's fine," he replied, "but just one question: are you the performance artist that I have been reading about all over the place? I saw a poster in Fort William about an unveiling tomorrow on the top of Ben Nevis – you've a long hike ahead of you in the morning if that is the case."

"How did you guess it was me?" he replied puzzled, not letting on that the event was on Slioch.

"Well it could have been the fact that you had to bend over almost double to get through the door, or the fact that you are completely naked apart from that dirty great feather stuck up your backside!"

"In that case, yes I am," he smiled. "Most people call me Icarus, but it's starting to wear a bit thin. My time alone as you will know yourself, has made me look deep into myself, and what I am seeing is very unsettling."

"Introspection... It's called introspection," added his anonymous bothy-buddy, "and it's a good thing; it's essential to our wellbeing and completeness."

"I am sure that you know of the Greek myth of Icarus and how he flew too close to the sun and that the wax holding his wings together melted and he plummeted into the sea and drowned"

"Of course I do," he replied, "a very special person gave me that name, because of my soaring spirit, as she told me, but I am beginning to doubt if I am worthy."

"Well, did you know that his father, Daedalus, was a fine craftsman and artist, and that he had designed and built a maze called the labyrinth for King Minos, the king of Crete? He had to keep captive a terrifying monster called the Minotaur. As it turned out, Daedalus betrayed the king, who had him thrown with his son into captivity in the labyrinth the unfathomable prison which he himself had created."

"I was a missionary for many years in South America, trying to feed the poor and save their souls. I knew a wealthy man there, who had amassed a fortune in mining opals in Australia. It was a mine that he had won on the turn of a card in a drunken poker game. To cut a story short he reinvested everything in palm oil and tripled his fortune."

"He was very generous to the poor natives, and we were able to feed and educate them. He made it possible for us to buy the medicines needed to treat the nasty tropical diseases that ravaged through the native villages with callous regularity. I always suspected that he was living his life as an act of contrition and one day, over a glass of uisce beatha,* he opened up his heart. He confessed that the man from whom he had won the opal mine, had a wife and two beautiful small children, and in a drunken

---

*   Gaelic: water of life, whiskey.

state after the game, he went home, took out a pistol and blew out their brains before turning the gun on himself."

"I always thought that he had come from a Greek family because he introduced himself as Tomás Daedalus, but he admitted that he was from County Mayo, and that he had left Ireland with his daughter in hard times to try and build a new life in Australia. He only moved to South America when too many Irish immigrants started asking too many questions about his Irish past."

"Apparently, he had taken the name Daedalus for two reasons: firstly, because he had built a prison or a labyrinth for himself that he could never escape. And secondly, because he had a son who had been nicknamed Icarus that he had abandoned along with his mother, when he had allowed the drink to destroy his life. The name Daedalus was some silly way of linking him to his son, knowing that he was not worthy or deserving of ever meeting him."

Icarus jumped up and bashed his head hard on the door frame, which seemed to make the receiving of the information a bit of a slapstick comedy, but in keeping with his life to date. He was conscious that he had an early start, but this was earth-shattering news to him.

"Can you tell me anything more about him?" he urged as he lurched forwards and grabbed him by the arms.

"Not much more Icarus, I never went to his home which I heard was a splendid place in the mountains above the tropical rain forest. I never met his daughter, nor his new wife. I don't think he wanted them to know about his philanthropy in case they suspected his guilt. Sadly his wife died of one of those tropical diseases that would not respond to any drug we had. He cursed the fact that he had so much money, and yet was unable to buy her an extra second of life."

"Over the years we often spoke about humanity, and religion and the end of things, but he was as many of us are, conflicted. He had a desperate desire to put things right, but felt he did not deserve the reward of doing so. He used to pray, believe it or not; more in the form of curses, but then his prayers became meditation and that benefitted him. He had an overwhelming need to help others, and I was astonished one day, when he agonised if there was any room in the church for a priest who thought that belief in God was a load of bollix."

Icarus looked bewildered yet spoke to him purposefully, "It seems strange that a man who won't tell me his name, has found me in a remote highland bothy, and seems to know a lot about a man called Tomás Daedalus and insinuates that he might be my father."

"There is more if you would like to listen," said the stranger.

"Firstly, I'd like to know how you found me," replied Icarus with a steely tone in his voice. "For years, I had a feeling that a man with a dog collar was shadowing me. Even when I was badly beaten I saw the shape of a man with a dog collar, but I thought it was all part of my fantasy world. Also some anonymous donor paid for my treatment at Slack-water House, and other kindnesses, that come to mind now. Was that man you?"

"For my sins, yes," he replied. "I was charged with the duty of overseeing your safety from a discreet distance, by a man who was filled with regret and shame."

"And how can I find this man... this Daedalus as you say he calls himself?"

"You won't find him," replied the stranger with compassion. "He does not want to be found: not even I know how he could be found."

Icarus's head was fit to explode with the possibilities that his father Tomás Gogarty was still alive. "But I was told that he perished in a storm off the coast of Achill..."

"He was never on that smuggling vessel," interrupted the stranger, "he had been tipped the wink by a Sergeant Fitzdick, who didn't mind doing a bit of illicit trade himself. It was all meant to be a diversionary tactic, but sadly the Sergeant lost his own son that night in the storm; he volunteered thinking it was going to be one big adventure. It suited your father, to be lost at sea," he added, "and after swearing his partners in crime to secrecy, the left the Island of Ireland, fully intending never ever to return."

Icarus, sat slowly down and then jumped up quickly to remove his rudder feather that had acquired an uncomfortable position. He was burning with anger, sadness, joy and longing all at once, and he could not speak. He lay down on the bottom bunk and pulled a blanket over himself as he handed his goose-feather over to the stranger. He then turned to face the wall and wept.

Come the morning, Icarus rose slowly and deliberately. As usual, he was not entirely certain if last evening had been a reality or a dream, or vice-versa. The stranger was gone, leaving not a trace behind him. Dare he imagine that his father was still alive? Did he have a sister, or half-sister, and if so, was she like him in any way? Would she like to have a strange, over-tall weird looking buffoon for a brother? He thought not, and he wrestled to clear such ridiculous ideas as were swimming round his head – and focus on the event of the day.

In the cupboard, previous guests had left a few scraps of food as is the friendly custom in the bothies, and he was able to make himself a little breakfast before he headed out for Slioch. It was already seven in the morning, and even with his enormous stride he knew it would be a good four hours before he reached its summit.

"There won't be a fecker there," he mumbled to himself, as he set off with his little rucksack and scruffy little suitcase. "But I'm going to do it for my own sake, if no one else's."

Donald Macleod's book described the route up to the top of Slioch as starting along the shore of Loch Maree, passing waterfalls and lochans and culminating in nice views from the summit. It was completely wrong in its description. He had only seen such beauty back in his beloved Ireland, but even that was being severely challenged. The waterfalls were stunning; the lochans were perfect; and the view from the top literally took his breath away. All of the strangeness of the previous day's meeting faded away. The magnificent beauty on that mountaintop filled his soul to overflowing.

"Yes, beauty does save the world – my world," he said.

A blinding flash that had him seeing purple spots, and a hearty slap on his back told him that Shay and Pappa had successfully scaled the Munro and were ready to set up their stall.

"I was a bit worried for a while," said Shay, still puffing from the strenuous climb, "but Pappa had no doubts at all. He said that an artist can recognise another artist, and that he knew you would not let us down."

Shay looked through his telephoto lens down to the shores of Loch Maree. "I think there must be one of those summer pop festivals going on down there. There are countless tents and thousands of people milling around. I hope that they don't interfere with our little extravaganza."

Over the next ridge a fully loaded highland pony was being led and making its way towards them. "Ah, that will be the plinth I had made. It's only plywood, put it's been painted to look like stone," said Shay. "I hope he was okay with the spelling though. I told him it was a famous sculpture by Rodin, and he growled, 'Who the feck's he?' I don't think he got my Irish accent, cos I kept having to repeat for him 'The Thinker' and he kept repeating back to me 'The Tinker?' and then I said, 'Listen, it's not "Tinker", it's "Thinker",' and then he said, 'What do you mean it's not "Tinker", it's "Tinker"! – I hope we don't end up with a display about a traveller that mends pots!'"

Meanwhile, over in Fort William, the local police were coordinating a group comprising the Irish Gardaí, Interpol and a hostile group of do-gooders and self-appointed keepers of moral standards. They had heard about Icarus's art installations and were determined to stop the one on the top of Scotland's highest and most iconic mountain.

"It would be an insult to God and the whole of Scotland," shouted one furious protester, who wielded a placard with the slogan: **'NUDITY IS SATAN'S WORK UNCOVERED!'**

Several hundred people were milling about, until some particularly pious looking woman blew a whistle and led them down the road towards Ben Nevis. They sang 'Onward Christian Soldiers' as they blew kazoos and rattled tin cans filled with dried beans. A couple of young lads joined in for a laugh and banged their big base-drums as though their lives depended on it. "What the feck's it all about?" one asked. "Who gives a fuck?" came the reply. "It's great – I never get to bang my drum like this in the middle of the day unless I am at a Celtic versus Rangers match!"

The Procurator Fiscal, much to his annoyance (it was his golfing day) had been told to attend in his official capacity, as had other prominent politicians and leading members of Scotland's hoi-polloi. No one knew for certain what to expect, apart from a team of ornithologists that had been drafted in from RSPB Scotland to help capture a rare and dangerous escaped raptor.

The team were in an animated discussion with a recent and most generous donor from Ireland called Doctor Mead, and a group of birdwatchers from the Social Services of Ireland.

"It's all set out and ready to fire, when the beaters have done their job," said the chief twitcher.* "We use rocket propulsion, to launch nets up and over the target. It's been used many times to catch large numbers of wildfowl on the Murray Firth for counting and recording flocks – it is remarkably efficient."

"But this rare bird, Doctor Mead, you say it's large; would it be haliaeetus albicilla, or perhaps aquila chrysaetus or something even more exotic like gymnogyps californianus?"

"No, it's so rare it hasn't been scientifically taxonomised as yet. It has an appearance of a gigantic pintail duck – anas acuta, to use your ornithological terminology, and appears to be the Irish subspecies of the continental stultus volantes icarusii."

The head twitcher was very impressed, assuming that Doctor Mead's doctorate was in biology and not in medicine. "So, it's new to science?" he chirruped and quivered with excitement.

"And that's why it's so important that we capture it, quickly and efficiently," affirmed the doctor. "But once caught, leave him up to me and my helpers to untangle him, he's very dangerous, and don't look him in the eyes, he'll hypnotise you like a king cobra and have your liver out for sure."

"So, it's a male then?"

---

* Ornithological jargon; a bird fancier who quivers with excitement on spotting something uncommon.

"Well, we're not exactly sure, it was reported somewhere that it could be an inbetweeny; but be very careful, he stands nearly seven feet tall and has a lethal tail feather."

The head twitcher started to worry. Perhaps he was putting himself and his fellow twitchers in peril. "Struthio camelus, stands ten feet tall, I know, but I don't like the sound of lethal tail feathers."

"What the feck do camels have to do with anything?" Doctor Mead demanded to know, growing in impatience.

"Struthio camelus... the common ostrich," he answered looking puzzled and starting to suspect that things weren't as they were being explained.

"Oh yes, yes of course, well you have nothing to worry about, like a stroo... camel... er ostrich or whatever, he can't fly either. His wings are only for decoration, and if you catch him first time, I'll double the amount on the cheque. You'll be able to buy fat-balls and sunflower seeds for a decade."

So, with that they all headed off for the slopes of Ben Nevis, and they took up their positions, hiding among the heather and peat hags before their quarry got wind of it.

High on Slioch, people in their thousands were making their way up to the summit for the three o'clock unveiling. Old-fashioned word of mouth had them coming, not just from all over Scotland and Ireland, but from all over Europe, the far East, North and South America and even Australia. It was an incredible sight and Icarus looked astonished.

"What the feck do they find alluring about a skinny-arsed bollix with a feather up his backside?" mocked the man with the highland pony, as he clumsily positioned the plinth.

"Be careful with that!" said Shay sharply, "That is to be part of an immortal work of art."

"Immoral, more like – and who gives a work of art the title of 'The Stinker'?"

"Oh no!" exclaimed Shay, "I knew your man would get it wrong."

"Hold on a minute; he had the phone on loudspeaker, I distinctly heard you say: 'It's not tinker, it's stinker!' And what

'The Stinker'

about the quote on the other side from that Des Cart fella, 'I Stink Therefore I Am', – I suppose that's wrong also?"

"Oh Jaysus!" said Shay, "And the curator from the Louvre is making a special trip out here!"

Icarus interjected: "I love it! – No, I really do! It's a continuation of my scatological installation. The next step: let's keep the title of 'The Stinker – I Stink Therefore I Am', everyone will relate to that. But no faecal matter this time, just symbolism; last time was all a bit stressful on my plumbing."

"Bravissimo!" agreed Pappa clapping, as he went to set up his tripod and select the correct lenses.

At that moment, Eva and the Macleods arrived with smiles as warm as warm could be. The twins had their pipes with them, and asked Icarus if he would like them to play for the unveiling. He was delighted to accept their offer and gave them a huge hug into the bargain. More and more people arrived at the summit and it all began to have a carnival atmosphere.

Meanwhile, back again at Ben Nevis, the protesters were becoming a little bored and restless. Nothing seemed to be happening, and the Procurator Fiscal pulled out his gold pocket watch that he had been given for a lifetime's service to the law, and huffed: "I would have been at the nineteenth hole by now!"

The local puritanical choir, began to sing half-heartedly 'Abide with Me', which triggered the drummers back into action like unexpected thunderclaps and frightened the singers half to death.

The twitchers mistook it for their pre-arranged signal from the beaters that stultus volantes icarusii was adjacent to the nets, and they hit the red button in an excited frenzy and fired the rockets. The nets soared skywards and across the target area, together with a random display of spare rockets that some idiot had carelessly tossed a cigarette-butt into. It was like a New Year's Eve firework display in the middle of the afternoon, and the whole gathering, mostly of self-righteous pensioners with their silly placards ran around squawking like startled chickens.

The biggest squawk came from Mrs Tapenade and the other members of her social workers' bird watching club. They wanted a front-row seat to view the capture, and had been unwisely crouching down in the heather, on top of the hidden net. The rockets had to be powerful enough to launch several hundred pounds of netting, and the extra weight of the ladies was no problem. As they flew across the sky, the drummers silenced their deafening beat in awe and wonderment: "Woa," they gasped, "they must be migratory birds – feckin' great fat ugly ones!"

They all landed with a splat in a soft peat bog relatively unscathed, but absolutely blathered in brown sludge. For all the world they looked like a fine example of poop art themselves. Mrs Tapenade was absolutely furious as Doctor Mead ran forward to offer some assistance.

"Did they catch him?" demanded Mrs Tapenade, "Don't tell me all of this was for nothing."

"I think he got away," he replied most apologetically, "those moronic twitchers let the rockets off far too soon before he was in position. He'll be miles away by now."

"Well that was a wild goose chase!" huffed the police inspector from Fort William to the various gathered authorities. "Where's that Doctor Mead, he's responsible for this debacle, I've a good mind to charge him with wasting police time and causing a public disturbance... indeed where is he?"

By the RSPB Land Rover, the crew were packing up their nets and trying to wrestle with Doctor Mead who was insisting on having his cheque back. When he saw a group of burly bemused Scottish policemen striding purposefully in his direction, he let go and dashed for his large silver Mercedes which was being revved up by his chauffeur ready for a quick exit.

"What about the ladies Doctor Mead?" he asked in concern.

"Feck 'em!" he sneered dismissively, "They're not sitting on my cream leather seats all covered in shite!" And with that, the chauffeur put his boot down and shot off at high speed imagining he was in some kind of Hollywood thriller. The old Ford escort police van chugged after them for about a mile with blue lights flashing, but soon gave up the chase, as opposed to Doctor Mead's chauffeur, who by then had turned into an intrepid rally-driver with all of the speed but not much of the skill. When they finally arrived at the ferry port of Stranraer, Doctor Mead was badly shaken, wondering where he could get his beautiful silver Mercedes valeted, with special attention paid to his cream leather seats.

In the public toilets Doctor Mead had gone through a whole towel roll and was attempting to dry his sodden soiled trousers by standing on his tiptoes with them halfway down his legs and his bare backside jammed up against the hand-drier. He could hardly bear the stench himself when he was interrupted by the strong arm of the law which gripped him firmly by the shoulder.

"Come along with us sir, nice and quiet now: indecent behaviour in a public lavatory is a serious offence!"

Back on Slioch, people ascended the mountain in droves. It was all incomprehensible to Icarus who readied himself by donning his performance dressing gown and sitting on the plinth where he was covered up by a large curtain as the countdown for three o'clock began. Eva poked her head through and gave him a wink, "I thought you'd like to know that a few of your old inmates have turned up from Slack-water House and Mr McTweezer wishes you the best of luck... you bollock-headed twat-arsed knob-end."

The twins began to fill their bagpipes with air, and Icarus's heart started to race as he took up the pose made so famous by Auguste Rodin. As the Skye Boat Song filled the air, Eva dramatically pulled the curtain back, like a matador's cape and revealed: 'The Stinker,' Icarus O'Toole in all of his artistic glory.

The applause was deafening, and the music was mighty as an army of musicians, many of whom had played at the last event, turned up for the craic. Pappa's camera flashed like the strobe lights in a disco, and everyone started to dance with joy.

"What brings you to this unusual arts event?" asked Shay in his capacity as journalist and chief project manager, to one young couple.

"Cos it's brilliant," they shouted as they got stuck into the 'tartan jive'. "No pseudo elitist arty-farty bullshit; just genuine shit... by and for the people!"

There were six Elvis impersonators; twelve Buddhist monks; a travelling troupe of circus performers and clowns from Budapest;

Chief Buffalo-whip of the Cherokee Indian Nation, plus three braves ; seven trawler men; three museum curators; one disillusioned catholic cardinal; a famous Russian opera singer (basso profundo); the entire cast of 'A Midsummer Night's Dream' on their rest day from the Eden Court Theatre in Inverness; Bridie Bremner and her entire flock of black-faced sheep, an Australian Aborigine on walkabout, and countless other folk all fascinated and wanting to see Icarus at first hand. Shay was busy counting the crowd and taking notes for his press releases when he was suddenly surrounded by the entire team of the Torridon Mountain Rescue.

"Who's responsible for all of this?" demanded the team leader.

"Well I suppose I am," confessed Shay expecting a telling off and a lecture about safety in the Highlands.

"In that case congratulations," he said as he thrust out his hand and shook Shay's firmly. "You know it's considered good safe practice to notify us of such a gathering in the Highlands, but I guess you weren't to know the response you'd get."

"I am astonished," replied Shay, "I only expected a dozen people at most. But I know with my experience as a journalist how news and rumour can spread like wildfire. And if you add in the effect of Chinese whispers, anything can happen."

"Exactly," said the team leader who was a tall athletic man in his early forties. "We had a call out to ensure the safety of a large group, who had come to the mountain to listen to the teachings of some kind of prophet and cult leader – according to the two o'clock news bulletin on Highland Radio."

"But how did they get the wrong end of the stick so back to front?" asked Shay.

"As you said, Chinese whispers; but I've heard about Icarus O'Toole from my younger sister, who's a great fan of his work. She wanted to go to art college, and on her application form she was asked which contemporary artists she admired, and she wrote down Icarus O'Toole. During her interview she was asked to explain her choice, and when she spoke of integrity and originality, four of the five interview panel asked her to leave immediately, describing him as an obscene charlatan. I know my sister well; she is rebellious, but with good instincts and is as honest as the day is long. As she left the interview, she turned and softly said to them: 'Ugliness is in the eye of the beholder, so you can all stick your degree where you all talk out of' – so now I'm a big fan too."

"Simply wonderful," said Shay, "Icarus will be delighted. Would you and your sister like to meet him?"

"She's over there already, making sketches of him and bombarding him with questions – but listen, I'd make a move to get everybody down from the mountain as a storm is on its way. You should be okay for about an hour or so, but I'd pack up now."

"My team and I will guide everyone down, showing them the safest routes, but there's another thing you should be aware of, a second more serious storm. I heard over my radio, that the riot police are on their way. Someone messed about with some powerful people in Fort William and they don't like being made fools of. Word got out about the real venue, and they're on the warpath, together with a full company of the Territorial Army."

Shay called Donald Macleod over who was having a great laugh with many of his Highland-games friends who had decided to combine the unveiling with a reunion. Shay told him the problem, and Donald instantly took charge.

"Okay lads, we're expecting a bit of bother, we need to get Icarus to safety. Everyone, clear the summit; Angus get the lads to form the Praetorian shield."

Just as in ancient Rome, the elite bodyguards known as Praetorians, were the inspiration for the eight massive Highland-game athletes. They had utilised the tactic successfully several times before when visiting dignitaries such as members of the Royal Family required safe passage, or referees from a Rangers and Celtic match needed to be rescued from the pitch.

The rain clouds began to gather a little earlier than had been expected and the wind began to roar as the Highland Praetorian guard began to march in the tight formation known as a Roman testudo, or tortoise, down the steep slopes of Slioch. All the while they were buzzed by a group of Japanese tourists who jumped up and down in their vain attempts to get autographs and snaps of their new pop idol.

"Tell 'em to feck off Donald, they're attracting too much attention; and Icarus, crouch down, that windmill cap of yours is a great giveaway. Mind you, we could make a bit of cash here – you're generating enough energy to run Edinburgh for a week in this gale."

"Aye agreed Donald, Ben Nevis has its hydroelectric power plant, why don't we install you on the castle rock in Edinburgh, for your next artwork extravaganza? We could call it 'Goon with the Wind', or 'Here Today, Goon Tomorrow'."

"What's with the goon?" complained Icarus and then added, "Goon but not forgotten!" They all laughed like hyenas.

"We'll need to fit cables though; strong enough to carry the electricity to the national grid," added Bruce Talisker. "And I'm well qualified as the 'current' shotput champion of Westmoreland."

"With a jack-plug, for correct connection up into the jacksie!" added Tam McBrae, claiming he was even better qualified as the current world champion heavyweight arm-wrestler and sparky by trade.

"Oh no, here we go again!" cried Icarus, doubling up in fits of hilarity.

"Good man, Icarus... now stay low," urged Donald as they struggled to keep in step and maintain the strict Praetorian Guard formation.

Unfortunately, the merriment and uneven terrain got the better of them all, and tripping about like puppets with tangled strings, they unwittingly revealed their charge to the advancing riot police and territorial soldiers.

"Remember Culloden!" shouted Tam.

"Och, you great toorie,* we weren't around in seventeen forty-six, and the Scots came second in that battle," mocked Donald.

---

* Scottish slang: the purple thistle, symbol of Scotland. A highlander's penis.

"Well remember Bannockburn then!" cried Angus.

"That was thirteen fourteen – but at least we won that one," shouted Bruce proudly, as if he were Robert the Bruce himself!

Most of the gathering had descended the mountain safely and were already in their camps, apart from a few hardy souls who were still on the summit dancing, singing and drinking, and smoking strange herbs with absolutely no intention of breaking up the party – until they noticed from on high that Icarus was in serious trouble.

They charged down the mountain joined by the rest of the gathering who had also seen the situation and surrounded Icarus in a confusion of bodies. He was advised to put on his corduroy suit to blend in with the crowd which he did as quickly as he could. The twins played a battle lament with all of their might which they then turned into a jolly Highland fling, and the tartan jive rallied to assist the crazy confusion that kept the authorities from picking up Icarus.

Captain Bombardier asked Inspector McNutter, what Icarus looked like and they both confessed to each other that they didn't have a clue; in fact, it seemed that no one really knew.

Interpol had sent a description of a tall naked man dressed in leather and feathers: "What kind of nonsense is this?" declared the inspector.

"He's either naked or no, and what's all this fetish leather and feather gear?"

"Wouldn't surprise me if he hadn't a whip. That sort always like whipping... yes, they enjoy it you know – the sweet pain." Captain Bombardier continued: "I remember one weekend on manoeuvres at Sandhurst; we had to crawl through three feet of mud for half a mile, while the colonel whipped and lashed us from above to toughen us up."

"Later, naked in the showers with our backs glowing and the hot steam rising, and everyone panting, the sense of comradeship and sheer pleasure of surviving the ordeal was exhilarating. Two spanking new recruits asked if they could go again for a second run. The bond was so strong that they ran out of the shower holding hands...! Ahem... well that's enough of that! Well I say it's all filth; a heinous corruption of decency, nothing less!"

Inspector McNutter looked at Captain Bombardier strangely and took a step backwards away from him. "Well we'll have to surround them all and bring a little order into the chaos in that case. Then we'll interrogate them all until Icarus O'Toole is identified. You know, I understand human nature, there's always some traitor in a crowd looking for approval from the authorities – mark my word!"

Captain Bombardier and his eighty soldiers, together with forty riot police, tried to shepherd the melee into some sort of order. It was like a sheepdog trial with untrained young dogs; eager – but all over the place. As soon as one area was contained, another broke free, all ably undermined by visitors from Slack-water House, and other like-minded folk. The straggly and bemused group chased in and out with great amusement as the music started up again as did the tartan jive. Captain Bombardier set his jaw firmly and thwacked his officer's whip into his gloved palm with eager anticipation.

"Ouch!" he whimpered, then smiled, "I'm going to enjoy this."

All the while, Pappa's camera was flashing as Shay wrote his account of the event for posterity but they were spotted by Inspector McNutter himself, who had them plucked from the crowd, dragged to the incident tent and cuffed. "What the feck's this?" complained Shay. "Freedom of the press; our human rights; we live in a democracy... freedom of expression and all that!"

"The truth of it is," snapped Captain Bombardier as he ducked into the tent, "is that in riot situations, martial law overrides civil law..."

"What feckin' riot!" demanded Shay, "this is a peaceful artistic event. Everyone is having a great time with not the slightest trouble – until you lot arrived and started throwing your weight around."

"I have my orders," insisted the Captain, "there are standards of moral decency that must be maintained, and from what I've seen, this gathering is an obscenity. There's nudity and drugs and pornographic dancing, and all kinds of filth here in abundance."

Then in trying to demonstrate his authority, he gave himself another smart thwack with his whip but missed the top of his boot and stung his lower thigh. "Ooh!" he moaned with a smiling grimace.

Unbeknown to the gathering, rent-a-mob had heard about the commotion and were eager to drag it into a war. They were a bunch of unemployed soccer fans who had been banned from their local clubs, and a drunken gang of bored jailbirds looking for amusement. Inspector McNutter had them bussed in from Glasgow to fuel the flames and to justify his heavy hand – and of course to make him look good.

In the field outside, a battle had indeed begun. Police dogs on tight leads were barking like crazy as the whole gathering descended into absolute mayhem. It was Bannockburn all over again without the English, in fact nobody really knew who they were fighting, but secretly they were all having a whale of a time, especially Donald and his pals.

Eva, was a great scrapper herself but stopped as she recognised the gang of jailbirds: "Jimmy, Sean, Eddy, Billy and the rest of you, what are you all doing here?" Eva had helped them all years ago when, like Icarus, she had helped them back into society. They all loved her to bits, and immediately stopped the kicking and fisting and ran to her, each hugging her in turn.

"Oh Eva, we've missed you. Life is so dull and boring since you moved on."

"Yes, but why and how did you get here?" insisted Eva.

Jimmy answered: "A bus was sent to pick us up from our estate. We were told they needed extras for a documentary that was being made about hooliganism in the Highlands and it was some kind of reconstruction that needed an element of reality; but feck me, those Highland boys are made of Cairngorm granite; I don't think anyone told them it was a mock battle."

As the gang sat down and began to swap tales with Eva, things began to quieten down. The bagpipes fell silent and the Forces instructed everyone to stay still and wait for instructions. Captain Bombardier could get neither sense nor information out of his two captives, so he strolled over to the now tranquil crowd to search for Icarus.

He carried an arrogant swagger in his walk, and he smacked the back of his boots with his whip in rhythm with his stride. He was staggered by the size of the crowd and he turned to his adjutant to get on the phone immediately to the Commando Training Centre in Fort William and request reinforcements.

"Summer madness, is what we'll call it," he shouted through a loudhailer. "You can all go home without being charged – and there were some serious goings on here that would justify custodial sentences – if you point out to me which one of you is Icarus O'Toole."

The crowd remained silent for what seemed an age as nervous glances darted about the crowd. Indeed, many of the crowd hadn't a clue what he looked like, or indeed who he was. "I'll give you one last chance, if Icarus O'Toole doesn't give himself up or is not identified, I'll remove you one by one in handcuffs and you'll face the full force of the law."

"Awa' ye bollix!" came a shout from within the crowd, "There's nae room for us all in the cells at Fort William."

"Find that man!" screamed the Captain, and a completely innocent man was briskly hauled out by three burly soldiers and clasped in handcuffs.

"Last chance," snarled the Captain as he cracked his whip into his open hand again. "Ow, wow... how do you think you can get away with concealing such a miscreant without suffering the dire consequences?"

Still the crowd remained silent. "Very well then you leave me no choice... Sergeant, on my count of ten, start taking them into custody."

When the count reached a nervous nine, a tall young man rose slowly and purposefully. With his hand held high and after a painfully long pause he asked: "What the feck's a miscreant?" and as a roar of laughter split the silence Icarus rose with great dignity to his feet: "I'm Icarus," he confessed.

Immediately another rose and shouted: "I'm Icarus."

"No, I'm Icarus," shouted another, and then another, until hundreds were standing and calling out that indeed they were Icarus. Even the twins got up and claimed to be him, as did their mother Tossa.

"Arrest every man who claims to be Icarus," ordered the Captain. "They'll wish they never spoke up by the time I've finished with them!"

"But some of them are women," said one soldier.

"Rubbish!" he cried, "And lipstick is no disguise to me. I remember one weekend at Sandhurst on manoeuvres...! Look, just arrest the feckin' lot of them." Captain Bombardier flexed his whip like a bow in eager anticipation of putting his interrogation skills to the test, but as he looked menacingly over his prisoners, it sprung out and smacked him hard in the eye.

Over in the office at the Commando Training Centre, Major Ince was spitting with fury. "Those bloody part-time toy soldiers are asking for what?"

"Reinforcements sir; they require assistance, some kind of riot on Slioch close to loch Maree. Someone reported a religious gathering on the mountain that has been spoilt by a streaker."

"And Bombardier can't sort it out as usual I suppose? He's as useless as a one-legged man in an arse-kicking competition. Get me the mountain rescue on the phone corporal, it's their kind of thing."

Captain Bombardier's adjutant, whispered into his ear, "The commandos aren't coming sir. Major Ince said something about kicking them up the arse yourself – but the line was bad, I think he said to be careful as prisoners have rights, and you may not have a leg to stand on."

When it transpired that the mountain rescue team had also been detained, Major Ince really lost it. "Tell that puffed up Bombardier, that if he doesn't take his thumb from out of his arse and stop sucking it. I'll pick half a dozen of my best men and teach him what real soldiering is."

The message was delivered with some amusement by the adjutant, who took charge and simply asked politely if people wouldn't mind going home. Inspector McNutter was a bit annoyed, but he was in no position to argue, so everyone just shrugged and set off home, apart from a hard-core of party goers who jived all through the night until dawn.

As it turned out Donald Macleod was a good friend of Major Ince and the next evening they sneaked over to the Commando Centre to meet him. The Major had seen him compete at the Highland games in his hay-day and held him in high esteem, for not even his fittest soldiers could match his sheer physical prowess.

"You should have joined us," he said as Donald and Icarus sat with him by the roaring fire in the Officers' Mess. "You'd have made a great sergeant major: commandos are fierce men and require strong leadership, someone they can admire and respect – not like that Bombardier ponce. But I hear that you retired from the games Donald, and that now you're a farmer and a family man – so how can I help you?"

Donald gave the Major a brief summary of Icarus's life, and the problem they now had in keeping Icarus safe. "Yes, Donald – quite a problem; it was on the national news this morning, and there were photographs splashed all over the newspapers. Apparently, heads will roll. So, in my official capacity, this meeting never happened, but as a friend I'll help you all I can."

"You'd both better stay with me tonight in my quarters, I'll just let the wife know... she's also an artist Icarus. I'm sure she'd appreciate some constructive criticism from a professional. She paints flowers and kittens and pretty things on glasses and milk bottles. She sells them in the local market and does quite well."

Both Donald and Icarus thanked him as they knew he was putting his neck on the chopping block, but he just smiled.

"Anything to fuck up that pompous Bombardier!" he replied and then explained: "He was supposed to provide logistical support for a group of trainee commandos on manoeuvres thirty miles from any road or town. The knapdarloch* dropped the supplies off a day late and at the wrong map reference point."

---

* Scottish slang: a lump of shit hanging from an animal's fur.

"It had been a dangerously hot day and the young lads were severely dehydrated, and without water two of them perished and the rest were hospitalised. When there was an inquiry, the milksop phoned his uncle, who's an Earl in the House of Lords, and it was all hushed up. So yes, I'm most definitely going to help you!"

"We'll follow the plan of The Young Pretender – Bonnie Prince Charlie himself. If you remember your Jacobite history, Flora McDonald disguised him as her serving-maid, and they successfully escaped from South Uist to Skye and then sailed to freedom in France. My commandos love adventure, and would enjoy the challenge of rowing over to France. We'll just say it's some kind of training exercise."

"Oh goody!" exclaimed Icarus, "I love dressing up in women's clothes, and will there be makeup?"

"That and a big red wig from the costume department at the theatre in Inverness; they promised to send some stuff over in the morning. My wife Jenny will play the part of Flora McDonald, and she'll help you with your makeup."

Icarus couldn't wait, and sure enough in the morning he and Jenny had a great time trying things on. They picked out the only dress that came anywhere near to fitting his six feet-ten tall figure. It had been designed for a magic trick, where one woman stood on the shoulders of another as part of the illusion, and thankfully it fitted – almost. The problem was the shoes: Icarus's size seventeen feet were an impossibility for the dainty high-heels that the theatre had sent. All that Icarus had that fitted were his enormous Doc Martin boots, kindly donated by his mysterious benefactor. When he put them on and hoisted his skirts to examine his ankles, they were all in hysterics.

"I said I was going to have fun!" proclaimed Icarus with a right royal curtsy.

FRENCH DRESSING

NE WEEK LATER, ON the northern shores of France, near the small Breton fishing village of Roscoff, Donald, Major Ince and his wife Jenny, bade a fond farewell to Icarus. It was half past midnight and he looked and felt like a vaudeville actress in the soft light of the crescent moon. His scarlet off-the-shoulder number and matching feather boa and lipstick had a burlesque feel to it. It inspired him and he burst into song as if he were rehearsing for an opening night at the Folies Bergère in Paris: "*Je ne regrette rien*," he wailed up to the moon, like an over the hill Edith Piaf with laryngitis.

"*Fermez la bouche s'il vous plaît!* Please to give les chats un chance," echoed a grunt from over the water. Icarus huffed and took out his compact mirror to check his lipstick when he was startled by a familiar flash. Pappa and Shay were walking down the harbour wall towards him, as had been arranged by Donald the day before, and taking snaps of him in his grandiose attire.

The next morning, over fresh coffee and croissants, Icarus, Shay and Pappa went over the project to date. They had booked into in a charming small hotel called Maxim's by the edge of the town.

"Do you still need to be in that dress?" said Shay as he stirred his coffee and tried to rescue a drowning mosquito from it.

"Do you not think it suits my complexion darling?" teased Icarus in a mock French accent. "*J'adore les vêtements Français!*" and he blew a kiss at him.

"Now stop that flirting..."

"Yes, I'm a flirt in a skirt."

"More like a mess in a dress if you don't pay attention to this. You don't want to miss the opportunity of performing up the Eiffel Tower in Paris!"

"I know where the Eiffel Tower is," replied Icarus with an air of nonchalance as he reluctantly dragged himself upstairs to change into his less-glamorous attire. After about an hour he re-joined them with a heavy sigh.

"Look," said Shay, "if you're getting bored, or losing your *raison d'être* to use your new-found lingo, just say so. I can think of a million things to do in this gorgeous place. The scenery is perfect, the restaurants are the best in the world, and the night-life lasts all night long!"

"Oh, I'm sorry," sighed Icarus. "I've been looking inwards far too much these past few days and have had little sleep. I always feel that I am being hunted by a dark monster who tries to suffocate me if I start to find a little peace, and last night it nearly got me. All of this artistic stuff – is it really me or am I just another pseudo bollix?"

"Now stop that nonsense right now!" urged Shay.

"*Si*, do the stopping of the feeling sorry for yourself," agreed Pappa, "we have the wonderful photos of your last events: we have the makings of a masterpiece publication, just a like Michelangelo!"

"You see, that's the crazy thing," said Icarus, "I'm nothing like Michelangelo, or Leonardo, nor any of the great artists who devoted a lifetime to learning their skill and then sacrificed and devoted themselves to their art."

"But Icarus," insisted Shay, "you have only done two major installations to date, and you have a huge following. You have inspired people to think again about artistic values and standards: 'What the feck is beauty?' is the contemporary question that everyone is asking."

"*Si*, also the peoples are saying, why should the snobbish few be telling us what a we should alike or a not alike?"

"I agree," said Icarus, "modern galleries are full of all kinds of rubbish and shite, arranged in a way that only the supposedly intellectuals and artists themselves can understand. It's all so much dressed up in psychobabble and jargon, that it is protected and isolated from the common people."

"If most people were to offer an old pile of bricks as a work of art, it would be dismissed as rubbish. If a celebrated artist did the same thing it would be called genius."

"Well that's it in a nutshell," added Pappa. "Your art shines a light on all that *caca*. None of the art criticals or professorial in colleges dare say *cazzate*✳ to the status quo for fear of being

———————— *"Je ne regrette rien"* ————————

✳ Italian slang: questionable truths expressed from the rear end of a male bovine.

having the piss removed. It's the old story of the emperor penguin's new clothes!"

"What the feck is the story of the emperor penguin's new clothes?" mocked Shay.

"Oh, every schoolboy in the world knows that one," said Icarus as he winked at Shay. "Down in snowy Antarctica, the chief penguin, known as the Emperor to his pals, was always complaining that he was frozen daft, and where his piles used to be, there hung icicles."

"His eightieth birthday was only two weeks away, so they all decided to have a whip-round, and buy him a warm coat. It was August and all of the charity shops were closed for the summer holidays..."

"Wait a momento, it's no summer in August in the southern hemi-spear," protested Pappa.

"Exactly," added Shay, "so you see how cold it had been!"

"Who's feckin' story is this?" said Icarus firmly and continued with a grin and a glare. "So with the money... well they don't have real money, not like us... but they do have credit-cards..."

"What a load of *coglioni!*"*

"No, it's true, I tell you; so, they waddled off – all six hundred of them, from their frozen colony to an ice-berg that was floating on its way to South Georgia, where they knew of a splendid coat shop. When they got there..."

"Oh, *Maddona mia!*"

"Yes, when they got there, they asked the tailor if he had a nice warm coat for a penguin, and the smart-arsed garsún wanted to know what was wrong with the traditional silver-paper wrapping. Indeed, they all agreed that the traditional classic fashion would be appropriate for their friend the Emperor."

"When they got home and on the day of his birthday, no one could find the silver wrap, cos some stupid bollix had left it floating away on the ice-berg."

"So what a did they do?" asked Pappa who was really getting into the tale by then.

---

*   Italian slang: balls that require a good kicking, but not as in football.

"Well, they gift wrapped an empty box, with fancy paper and ribbons and all..."

"Bought from the Antarctic stationers, off the top shelf – the ice-shelf I suppose," interrupted Shay trying not to laugh.

"Well, as it happens – yes. They were all huddled together in this massive ice storm and blizzard, and no one could see a dickie-bird. The Emperor was nithered half to death, so they handed him the box and wished him a happy birthday. Of course, he couldn't see in the blizzard, and he assumed his present had blown away as he unwrapped it, but not wanting to embarrass himself nor disappoint his friends, he thanked them regardless."

"Later that day, he was seen wandering about the colony with his head poking through a hole he had made in the top of the box. 'Best feckin' coat I ever had,' he squeaked as he waddled on his way into the fierce wind. Everyone told him how wonderful his new coat was and how it suited his figure and colouring. 'Stupid lying twats,' he squawked to himself, as he skidded across the ice.

'Stupid old twat!' his friends squeaked back when he was out of earshot."

"So, I think we can all agree," said Shay, "that things are perceived differently by different people."

"*Si, si*, but what happened to his feckin' coat?"

"That's the point, there never was a coat," said Icarus.

"*Si si*, of course there was," insisted Pappa. "The gonzos left it ona the ice-berg."

Shay turned his eyes up to the heavens, then took a big slurp from his coffee, and thanked the heavens that Pappa was an excellent photographer.

Icarus started to laugh and his spirits lifted, as the others joined in. Then they decided to reconvene later that afternoon and Icarus got up first intending to go up to his room for a lie-down and a think. As he passed reception on the way up to his room, the concierge handed him his mail. There were a surprising number of letters and back in his room he threw them untidily onto his bed and started to open them.

They were mostly fan mail and letters of support, some with donations, but the one that caught his attention had been redirected from Slack-water House. It had a postmark and stamp from Suriname in South America, with a beautiful butterfly on it. The letter looked equally mysterious and precious, and he held it gently in his trembling fingers, far too nervous to open it. "Not now... later," he whispered to himself with his heart thumping in his breast. He carefully placed it against his dressing-table mirror and eventually went downstairs to talk further with his friends.

He joined the others in the lounge and sat down in an old creaking wicker chair. He expressed his worries about the number of letters that had so easily found their way to him.

"Don't worry about that Icarus," said Shay reassuringly, "that's just Eva doing a great job, she has set up a mailbox number for you in Dingle and has spread the word. She just bundles the letters together and sends them out here. The envelope has only the manager and the hotel address on it, with a note inside to pass everything on to you. Your secret location is safe."

"Well that's a relief," puffed Icarus as he tried to relax into the rickety chair. "Look, I've been thinking about everything and I'd like to continue with the installations, and Shay you write about them, and with Pappa's marvellous pics, I'm sure it will make a great artbook. But when it's done, I'm done."

"Oh Icarus, you'll be the toast of the free-thinking world. You'll be a celebrity, even bigger than you are now. You'll be invited to open bridges and important supermarkets. You'll be on every chat show there is! Don't stop when it's really only just beginning. You could really make a difference."

"Ah don't *plámás** me Shay, my mind is made up. When I first came out of Slack-water House, I was clueless. Eva was a great friend to me, and she helped me to fill a huge gap in my life. I've always been away with the fairies, and it suited me. I was even sincere about being a performance artist, but the fan-mail and the celebrity status is just bonkers."

"I read avidly as a boy, and remember reading a critique on art. It described the pursuit of excellence and perfection as the pinnacle of man's or woman's ambition. Creation should be a

---

* Gaelic: to flatter, to spread the Kerrygold thickly.

holy thing, not in a religious sense, but it should engender wonderment and a great feeling of belonging to something greater than we are: civilisation and its partner humanity in all its nobility if you like."

"It takes years to build anything of worth, but it takes just a second to knock it down. It is much easier. There can be excitement in demolition, I admit, but it is the lazy way, and it falls a million miles short of the fulfilment given to the achievement born of a lifetime's dedication."

"I fear that my art takes only moments to make, and it'll be hanging around for years in that book of yours. Oh, guys, I just don't know anymore! The perfume of a rare and delicate rose is fleeting, but equally, so is the stench of one of Pappa's farts – yes you Pappa; I followed you into the loo this morning and had to back out of there for a good half hour!"

"*Scusami*, but the French olives always do it to me!"

"Ah don't apologise, Pappa. I left it in a much worse state after you. I notice that half a dozen scent candles are burning in there now. But seriously, everything is an enigma to me; everything is nonsense. Beautiful things that should have been in my life have faded like the perfumed rose, and what am I doing? I'm replacing them with one of Pappa's farts."

"Donna blame me," complained Pappa, "Next time I go for the caca, I burn the match. You a try it Icarus – it burns away the marsh gas."

"Jaysus!" exclaimed Icarus, "If I struck a match, I'd blow the whole shitter down!"

"Oh yes, that reminds me," said Shay, "there was a letter in the *Irish Times*, from some politically correct art critic. Don't know her name, but she was berating your art. She said that you are intellectually, emotionally and ethically bankrupt, but her biggest criticism was that none of your installations was carbon neutral, and that your carbon footprint is irresponsibly huge."

"Is a bigga lie," said Pappa in his friend's defence, "he's a very vertical signor; he needs extra bigga shoes or he a fall over."

"I'll reply to the editor," said Shay, "he actually is a good friend of mine. I'll point out that you have a renewable energy head, and that you'll plant a tree in your own homemade manure at every installation. I knew him when we were students together and he's a wicked sense of the ridiculous. He'll be up for helping you I'm sure!"

"That's great," replied Icarus, "so starting with the Eiffel Tower, could you guys work out a time-plan and identify all the places we are going to visit. You know my ideas about world famous iconic sites, but I'll leave it up to you. We have plenty of money to get about and pay for accommodation and stuff; for some reason the cash keeps flooding in."

With that he tried to stand up intending to go upstairs and open his letter, but the rickety wicker-chair seat had sunk and snatched tight hold of him round his backside. "What is it with me and my arse!" he sighed as it absolutely refused to release his buttocks.

After a Herculean struggle that had everyone in stitches, and with the help of the concierge, they managed to kick the chair free. "Jaysus; that chair has a bite like a crocodile," he panted.

"Will you gentlemen be dining with us tonight?" asked the breathless concierge, "And Mrs O'Toole – will she be joining you?"

Icarus was halfway up the stairs when he glanced at himself in the gilt mirror hanging there. He took a closer second look and noticed that he hadn't removed the scarlet lipstick. The concierge who was grinning up at him, gave him a sly wink, and pursing his lips he purred: "*A bientôt ma chérie.*"

Back in his room, he sat down on his bed with his letter and smoothed out the wrinkles in his dress He loved wearing it; the floating material and the feel of synthetic silk against his skin. The intense scarlet flooded him with excitement and he wondered why men's clothing were so drab. It had felt like a real downer when had taken it off, and so he dreamily pulled his dolly out from under his pillow and asked, "What do you think Daisy?"

He looked again at the beautiful butterfly on the stamp before opening the letter and mused that butterflies know exactly how to dress. Then, quickly like pulling a sticking plaster off a cut, he ripped it open as if to shorten the pain. The letter had no address nor date on it, and it began:

Dear Timmy,

I knew your father many years ago and it has been many years since I saw you, in fact you were just a baby. I also knew your mother, but I was not a good friend to her I am ashamed to say. I heard that she had died some years ago and I am deeply sorry for your trouble.

I have been living overseas for many years now and have done well, but for all kinds of reasons I have found it difficult to return home to my native Ireland, which has always saddened me. I learned of your accident and injuries from someone who knew you well, and it was I who organised the fees due to Slack-water House.

The priest whom you met recently has been watching over you from a distance, and that is how I have been kept informed about you. You may ask what have I to do with you. Well the answer is simple really: as a young man in Ireland, I did many wrong things, some because I was so poor, but I have to confess, I did many stupid things because simply I was a young pup. I could have helped you and your poor mother but I did not – I was far too selfish then. I have the wealth now to try and correct some of those wrongs, but to my sadness I find that money cannot change the past, nor buy many of the things that I desire.

I have a terminal illness, and I do not know how long I have left, but before I die, I would like you to know that I have left you the bulk of my wealth in my will. I know the kind of man you are, and I would hope that you would use the money wisely to do good.

I also have a daughter that I would like you to meet, but she will not leave my side. She feels that she can make me better, but in my private conversations with my doctors I know there is no hope for me.

*I wish you every success in your artistic endeavours,
and I feel sure you will shine a light on those dark hidden
corners of ignorance and greed.*

*With deepest affection,
A well-wisher.*

Icarus stared at the wall, not knowing what to think. He even wondered if it was a sinister joke, or some kind of con where he would have to send money to a bogus solicitor to have the funds released. "That's it he said; word has got out that I have the sponsorship money, and some begrudger or other wants to get his hands on it!"

He carefully placed the letter back in the envelope and leant it back against the dressing-table mirror and continued with his other mail. There was a most welcome letter from Eva, who said she was coming out to Brittany to join them. She had news about all kinds of things and wanted to catch up. She also fancied a cycling holiday away from it all, and the terrain was nice and flat there. Icarus smiled to himself, as he knew her wicked sense of humour well. She asked if he wanted her to bring his favourite bike from the Macleods so that he could join her.

After at least a hundred letters, he had had enough, and he stretched out on his bed and decided to have a little nap before dinner. His feet stuck out uncomfortably but he soon dropped off cuddling his little dolly tightly in his arms.

His sleep was restless however, and he had strange dreams of being chased and not being able to run away. He could see his mother in the distance calling out to him with outstretched arms, and a horrible little man stalking her from behind, and when he tried to call out to warn her, nothing would come out. At eight o'clock precisely, Icarus was woken by a light knock on his door. It was Shay who told him that dinner was at nine, but they were meeting in the bar at eight-thirty.

At half past eight on the dot, A glamorous figure swept down the staircase in a stunning scarlet dress and feather boa, with all of the confidence and swagger of a Hollywood film star. Then a burlesque type voice with a ridiculous French accent declared:

"Monsieur Concierge, please take note that Mr O'Toole will not be dining with us *ce-soir!*"

Pappa nearly fell off his seat, but he had the presence of mind to take some wonderfully stylish photographs of Icarus in full flow descending the stairs. "Good enough for a Vogue magazine front cover," he declared with pride.

"Certainly is," agreed Eva, who rushed up to Icarus and gave him a huge hug as she wrestled with his feather boa. "I told the others not to say that I would be here this evening – nice surprise, *n'est-ce pas?*"

"*Mais oui, ma petite chou-fleur,*" replied Icarus. "I am most *enchanté* that you are *ici.*"

"Oh, for feck's sake," laughed Shay, "I have enough trouble with Pappa's Italiano. Let's stick to English – you know a Sassenach once told me that God intended for the whole world to speak English – and he insisted that it was proven by the fact that the Bible is printed in English!"

"Bollix, but I'll drink to that!" cheered Eva, who had ordered a bottle of the finest champagne. The concierge entered with a silver bucket filled with ice as he peeled the foil from the neck of the bottle.

"I'm also the sommelier," he announced with pride as the cork exploded up into the cut-glass chandelier and sent the crystals showering down upon their heads.

Pappa picked up two of the pear-shaped prisms and held them up to Icarus's earlobes. "Just alike Gina Lollobrigida," he insisted. "Give to me a kiss."

"Give tummy a kiss?" mimicked Icarus as he towered over Pappa. "What's a wrong...? Can a you no reach my lips?"

With that, everybody, including all of the other hotel guests, fell about laughing, and that set the tone for the whole evening. The champagne flowed as did the jokes and horseplay, and at midnight, the small jazz-band that always played on a Friday night, made sure it was one they would never forget.

Icarus danced the Argentine tango with Eva all through the restaurant out into the street around the harbour and back again. They had been joined by an out of control hen party who couldn't find their hotel; a dozen or so members of gay pride who ended up in the wrong town and missed their protest march; and two starving stray dogs who could smell food but couldn't find it. It all descended into a wild conga dance and Icarus insisted that everyone must dance, and off they went around the harbour again and then followed the bright lights into the town like moths around a candle-flame.

On a small table outside of the hotel, a small but portly man was sucking on a smelly fat cigar as he was being served a cognac by the concierge. "Who's the tall good looking broad in the red dress?" he asked.

It was six o'clock in the morning before anyone arrived back at the hotel. They came in dribs and drabs in various states of disarray, all but Icarus who arrived in style, sitting proud and high on top of a magnificent ebony carriage, pulled by two plumed black horses. As he dismounted, he wrapped the feather boa around the driver's neck and gave him a huge embrace. "*Un petite cadeau pour vous* to remember *moi*," he smiled and kissed the palm of his hand and blew him a huge kiss, and then dashed up to his room to shower and change.

The carriage door opened and the remainders of his new-found friends tumbled out all tangled in balloons and streamers and clinking with empty bottles. The local priest who had been at the home of a bereaved family giving the last rites, somehow latched on to them and was now slumped on the pavement. He managed to sit upright with his legs splayed out in front of him and he slowly attempted to pour himself a glass of wine. His hopeful grin faded however, as the tipping bottle reached vertical without yielding a single drop.

"*Mon Dieu!*" he cried, "*Quelle heure est-il?* I have to take *la cérémonie funèbre de Monsieur Mangetout. Le cortège commence à neuf-heures précisément.*"

"Not to worry," replied Icarus dressed once more in his more conventional attire, "and we'll all come with you, won't we?" and a drunken cheer rose from the tangled bodies on the pavement as they immediately piled back into the carriage.

"Where the feck are we going now?" slurred one of the gay pride members.

"I'll be fucked if I know, blathered his fellow reveller."

"Ooh, you smooth talking bastard!" he grinned as he stared back into his bloodshot eyes.

"*Non, non, mes amis*, you must be getting out. I must to the funeral go, we must have some decorum."

"Can you understand him?" said one.

"I think we have a choice of either dick or rum," said another.

"Sounds like my kind of party!" roared a third… "What are we waiting for… *allez, allez!*"

"But you are all dressed as for the party, you will need *les chapeaux noirs* for the funeral."

"Not to worry *mon ami*," said Icarus, "we'll stop at a gents' boutique on the way and get togged up properly. If French funerals are anything like Irish funerals, we'll be in for a great time!"

The priest known locally as Père Paul, began to sober up as they approached the home of the Mangetout family on Rue Victor Hugo. "Didn't he write *The Hunchback of Notre Dame*?" asked the one remaining girl from the hen party as she spotted the road sign. "Seems to ring a bell!" replied Icarus as the others hooted and jeered at him.

Père Paul began to realise his folly as the Mangetout family were highly respectable members of the Roscoff community. The funeral was to be held at the splendid church of Notre Dame de Croatz-Batz, and it was meant to be a sombre affair.

Just opposite the Maison Mangetout, Icarus spotted a gentlemen's boutique, much to the relief of Père Paul, and they all scrambled out to try to buy a respectable black hat each. Icarus stayed with the priest, hoping to reassure him of his friends' behaviour as they risked their lives crossing over the busy road to the boutique.

"Who speaks French?" one of them asked as the little bell on the door tinkled and the shopkeeper came out to attend to them. One of the gay pride party pushed himself forwards, still as drunk as a skunk, and insisted that he should translate because for years he used to smoke Gauloises cigarettes.

"*Nous* – that's us, *désiré* to *attendons le funerallez au jour* doowee." He swayed and looked back at his partners in crime for approval and continued with a grin: "*Avez-vous les*, err... les... hey what the feck is French for hat...? Oh yeah, *avez-vous pour* us *ici, une capote** *noire* so we can *donner* respect *avec la* bereaved *famille triste*?"

"*Ah, non monsieur, il vaudrait mieux chercher une pharmacie!*"

On their way out, tripping over each other, their French translator declared: "By his accent I think he was Algerian or something, because he struggled to understand my Parisian French. I think it must be similar to how they sell stamps here in France at the tobacconists; they appear to sell hats at the chemists."

As luck would have it there was *une* pharmacie on the opposite side of the road and they narrowly avoided certain death in trying to cross over. "Leave this to me," insisted the self-appointed translator. "So how many hats do we need? One, two, three, err, um, six, seven; yes, seven hats of the colour black – back in a jiff."

At the chemist's counter he was confronted by a humourless man in his late sixties whose only word to him was, "Oui?"

"*Mes amis et moi desiré attondons un funeral. Pour donner le respect exactement, nous voudrai acheter les capotes noires, s'il vous plait.*"

"*Oui.*"

Then his wife who spoke a tiny bit of English butted in out of curiosity. "Would *les messieurs* prefer *les capotes* ribbed, vibrato, or flavoured *comme les fruit*?"

"*Si vous plait, noir.*"

"*Ah oui, c'est le cassis,** *et combien de?*"

"Oh, *je pense seulement* seven... err *sept. Est-ce que tous le* same size... err?"

"*Le mot...* err the word for size is *taille*," she giggled as she started to see the funny side of it all.

"*Mais oui, nous...* that's us, *sont les* sizes, err *tailles différents, naturellement. Personnellement, mon taille est* nine and three quarters."

---

*   French colloquial: condom.
*   French: blackcurrant.

"*Naturellement!*" she agreed pursing her lips. "*Vous êtes un* big boy!"

"*Ah oui, mais deux* of *mes amis sont* much more *grandes. Mon ami* Bernie's *taille* is ten and seven eighths."

"*Mon Dieu!*" gasped the pharmacist's wife, "*Vive la différence!*"

"*Oui!*" he agreed, "*Vive la France!*"

"*Mais*, not to be worry," she reassured him, "*les capotes* they are stretching to fit all *tailles.*"

The gay pride member whose name was Lionel, worked on a checkout counter at his local supermarket back in Swindon. He was starting to swell with pride at his articulation of the French lingo and his newly attained status and responsibility.

"*Et maintenant, vous avez trois* – that's three for each of you *dans le paquet*," she informed him.

"*Pourquoi?*" replied Lionel looking confused.

"*Parce que*, it is of the possibility one might burst when you put it on, *n'est-ce pas*. A real *gentilhomme* always has one *dans le* back-pocket in reserve."

"Well fuck me down our lane and back again," gasped Lionel, "that's new... how much will that... err *combien d'argent y a t'il?*"

"*Pour vous, absolument rien...* nothing. *Un cadeau* from France to you all. *Préféreriez-vous le* wrapping *comme un cadeau?*"

"*Mais non!*" he insisted triumphantly. "*Nous donner on notre* heads *immédiatement.*"

Madame Soupçon, the pharmacist's wife handed over a small carrier bag with a smile. "*Incrédules, les Anglais. Vous avez beaucoup de respect, n'est-ce pas!*"

As Lionel bumbled out of the chemists, Monsieur Soupçon asked his wife why she had given him les capotes for free.

"*Je l'ai fait parce que*," she replied, "*nous ne devons pas permettre à ces imbéciles de se reproduire avec nos filles Françaises. Nous ne pouvons risquer une génération de crétins!*"✳

"*Oui!*"

✳   French: our French girls would make an intelligent match for our English allies.

Still swaying from the drink, Lionel miraculously managed to avoid the frantic French rush-hour traffic, and he fell into the carriage with his small carrier bag and joined his friends.

"Are they all in that little bag, Lionel?"

"*Mais oui.*"

"Cut the Franglais crap! There can't be seven hats in this little bag"

"They're French: small and bijou – apparently they stretch. One size fits all," explained Lionel, "and I did get 'em for free!"

Père Paul grabbed the bag and looked inside suspecting that something had gone awry in the translation. "*Quelle horreur!*" he gasped, "Please to remove from the hearse yourselves and this disgusting little bag *immédiatement*. The coffin *de Monsieur Mangetout* will be here *en un moment, avec le* grieving *femme et membres de la famille.*"

"Not to worry," said Icarus, "I'll get them out of here, but perhaps we could follow you to the church service and join in with the hymns. We all like a good sing-song, and maybe we could join you all at the wake and help lift everyone's spirits."

After the coffin of Monsieur Mangetout had been placed into the hearse and the family had been organised, it set off at a gentle pace towards L'Église de Notre Dame de Croatz-Batz, with Icarus's party straggling loosely behind. They resembled a group that hadn't read the invitation properly, and had turned up to an important black-tie dinner in fancy dress.

"Everyone's looking at us," said Lionel.

"I wonder why," puzzled Icarus as he brushed the party streamers and spent balloons from his shoulders.

One of the cortège asked who they all were, and Père Paul who was driving the coach and horses, informed them that they were his pallbearers. Icarus turned to his friends and announced with a flourish, "*Mais oui certainment, nous sommes* the Father Paul bearers!"

Icarus and his friends slumped at the back of the church in various states of consciousness, some snoring, some trying to sing like Luciano Pavarotti, and others just desperate for another drink. After a solemn and dignified service, they all bowed

their heads and joined the family line and to shake hands with everybody.

At funerals in France, it is not unusual to have unknown guests appearing out of the blue. It is explained by the fact of the French predilection for illicit and nefarious affairs with, but not always, members of the opposite sex.

It was assumed that Icarus's party fell into that category, and once word spread, they were welcomed with open arms. The wake was a magnificent affair, held at the Mayoral Palace on Rue de la Maison Cul. The wine flowed in rivers and everyone dived in for a swim. Icarus scrambled back to the hotel at two in the morning and eagerly put on his scarlet dress. He was followed back to the wake by the small American guy, with the smelly fat cigar. He was fascinated by Icarus as he sailed onto the stage and gave them all the full theatrical works that he had perfected at Slack-water House.

"Geez, that gal's a star," he gasped as he pushed his way through to the stage holding out his business card. It read: 'Solly Lieberkraut, theatrical agent, New York, London and Paris.'

He was just about to climb the stage and present it when Lionel swept him up in his arms for a dance. The more French wine he had drunk, the bolder his French became. He grabbed Solly towards him by the waist and said, *"J'adore les petites chubby hommes Américaine. Voudrez-vous coucher avec moi ce soir?"*

Solly's response was to knee him right in his family jewels, and he sunk to his knees with a grunt. "Fucking slimy pervert!" he spat as he attempted to mount the stage once more, but he was swiftly dragged back by the collar by the other gay pride members who always looked out for each other.

"Take that, you homophobic *homme!*" they screamed as they gave him a vigorous and humiliating bitch-slapping.

"Geez, I only wanted to talk to the broad. Can't go anywhere these days without having to keep your ass backed up against the wall, those fucking Nancy boys are everywhere. Well we are in France, so I suppose..."

"Qu'avez-vous dit?" said Père Paul who was fully fuelled up again on Chateau-Neuf-du-Pape.

"*Oui; qu'est-ce qu'elle a dit?*" demanded a pissed up and pissed off gathering of nationalistic French funeral followers.

"Look," apologised Solly looking very worried, "I only wanted to talk to the gorgeous broad. I'm a famous Hollywood producer. I could do big things for her!" and he whispered to himself: "Yeah, great big things – especially with this big beast in my pants!"

Icarus could see the jostling going on and he climbed down from the stage to investigate and see if he could calm things down. He very quickly picked up on the situation and seductively lassoed Solly Lieberkraut with his feather boa and teasingly dragged him over.

"Gee thanks Miss... er Miss... I was in real trouble there! Nice to be in the arms of a real woman!"

Icarus pulled him close and grinned at his friends over his shoulder. He intended to have a bit of fun.

"So, you're a single broad then, Miss... Miss... I didn't catch your name?"

"That's because I didn't throw it darlink," replied Icarus in a strange eastern European accent, reminiscent of Zsa Zsa Gabor on speed.

"I just love the accent babe, but hey – no need to play hard to get!" he replied as he struggled onto his tippy-toes to blow in Icarus's ear. "I've been watching you since you came to stay at Maxim's – hey that weird tall guy – he's not your husband, is he?"

"Not to worry darlink, he's very liberal; we like to enjoy the open rela-tionships. No jeal-ousy; we are free to

Solly Lieberkraut

159

take lovers any time we like. But kiss me, I feel the passion rising in my breast and correct me if I'm wrong, you wild man – it also rises in your trousers."

"Well I think I'll have to climb up on this chair to reach – geez, are all the broads as tall as you in your country?"

"It's the river Danube that flows with deepest passion through beautiful Budapest, my home. It is so fertile, it surges with life and desire my darlink. You know there are many women much taller and more bountiful than I in Hungary, and it drives all the men crazy!"

Solly thought about it and said, "Well I suppose it's no problem as you broads are more or less the same height when you are lying down on your backs – if you get my drift – everything's within easy reach!"

"Oh, you naughty darlink!" gasped Icarus as he slapped him hard on his back.

"Ow!" complained Solly, as he staggered forwards and buried his face in Icarus scarlet dress, and almost swallowed his cigar.

"So, what about that kiss darlink?" teased Icarus. "You must not lead a girl on and then disappoint her... but I think you'll need a tall chair – perhaps the barstool over there?"

Icarus waltzed Solly towards the bar and deliberately kicked his shins with his Doc Marten boots at every turn. He then bounced him up onto the barstool with his enormous powerful hands and pursed his scarlet lips. Solly was able to have a good look at his dance partner for the first time, being on the same level, and he screwed up his face in horror. Under the thick grease paint, he could clearly see a small moustache and dark prickly stubble.

"What's the matter darlink?" mocked Icarus as Solly shrieked and dived off the stool crashing into a stack of empty bottles behind the bar. The whole funeral party erupted in hilarity as the high and mighty Solly Lieberkraut had been brought crashing down to earth.

"You dancin' Icarus?" asked Eva in her usual direct manner. She had searched for him all over the town and had found him when a local Gendarme told her where he was. They had been called out three times to tell them to keep the noise down, and when they had no success they all just joined in, as did the complaining neighbours. Monsieur Mangetout had been much loved in Roscoff, and it was to be a send-off that no one would forget and probably few would be able to remember.

The celebration of his life went on all night and all of the next day. In order to continue, it was necessary to send to the nearest town to replace the exhausted supply of wine, and when that supply ran out, they had to request a delivery from the enormous wine-export warehouse in Calais.

Not caring if they lost their jobs, the deliverymen refused to drive back to Calais. They joined in as did the whole of the town, including Pappa and Shay who had followed the sound of the uproar. Thanks to Icarus, it had been a truly crazy momentous and wonderful wake, and afterwards the whole town hugged and thanked him, then trundled wearily home to sleep it off.

After a very long sobering-up snooze, Shay, Eva and Pappa joined Icarus for coffee at the little outside table that Solly Lieberkraut favoured. "Where's the little American guy?" they all asked the concierge.

"Oh, he's on a plane flying back to the States. He'd spent the night at the hospital in casualty having his head patched up. He'd somehow ended up in the wrong side of town and got bottled for his trouble; and to add insult to injury, on his way home he was mugged by two guys disguised as nuns. So, as we say in France: *'Il n'était pas un lapin ravi!'* or as you would say; he was not a contented bunny!"

They all tucked into their croissants and coffee and recounted the fun they had at Monsieur Mangetout's wake. Shay asked the concierge if that was normal for towns in Brittany.

"Mais non!" he replied, "Roscoff would be bankrupt very *rapidement*, and a lot of peoples would be dead before their time! It's you, monsieur Icarus, you are the life and soul: everywhere you go you bring joy."

"Not to mention the chaos!" grimaced Icarus.

"A joyful chaos Icarus," confirmed Shay detecting a sombre tone in his friend. "So much of life has a strict rigid order that makes day to day living lose its happiness. Yes, Icarus, you bring a joyful chaos to everyone's lives."

"That's what I cannot reconcile. I only seem to be okay when everything is crazy around me. I need the madness to keep me from going insane. All of my life has been that way. If I see that my days are becoming 'normal' I become restless. I put flowers upside-down in vases and pretend that's how I thought it should be done. Not too reckless really, unless you happen to be a nice bunch of roses!"

"My stay here with you in France has been wonderfully bonkers, but it has shown me how out of balance I really am. I have accepted that I am strange, but there is a longing deep inside of me that I just cannot satisfy. Something is missing in me, I have an empty space that echoes to me in the dark of the night – and I am unable to rest my weary head."

He took out from his inside pocket his letter from Suriname and showed it to Eva who then showed it to the others. "Somewhere I have a father that I believe is still alive, and perhaps a sister. The point is I have family that I must find, and I am sorry Shay and Pappa, I cannot go on any further with you."

"Eva, you have been a wonderful friend to me and I love you dearly. Please if you could, look after my interests back in Ireland, and continue to shine a light on Doctor Mead and his cronies' antics. They'll get their comeuppance for sure."

"But where and how will you...?" Eva could hardly speak for choking up with tears.

"I will be heading for South America to trace the steps of my father. I do not know where it will lead me, but it's where I will start. I had another letter from a solicitor based in Scotland and I am entrusting it to you Eva. I have included my bank details in the envelope because it contains a cheque for forty million dollars. You know I'd swap every cent in a heartbeat just to see my father once, or to turn the clock back to rescue my dear mother and my lovely Daisy Maisie."

Everyone at the table was absolutely stunned into silence, and they all stood up and hugged him with tearful eyes. Icarus found it impossible to turn back to wave at them as they drove away in the taxi he had booked earlier, and he whispered to himself: "Broken-hearted if I leave and broken-hearted if I stay."

They all stood up and watched the taxi for as long as it was possible and until it finally disappeared out of sight. They were trying to hang on to him for as long as they possibly could, and no one spoke for ages.

"What kind of man with so little, leaves forty million dollars behind to chase a hopeless dream?" asked Shay.

"A great man; an extraordinary man, and a man of honour... Icarus O'Toole... that's who," declared Eva with pride.

As the taxi sped off towards Charles de Gaulle airport in Paris, the flashing lights and sirens of two police cars screeched to a halt on the pavement in front of the hotel, and almost crashed into their table.

"Nobody move; we have a European warrant for the arrest of the criminal who goes by the name of Icarus O'Toole. We have information..."

"*Quel dommage* officers, he's not here, he checked out last night," interrupted the concierge. "He's on his way to Morocco to do a performance of 'Laurence of Arabia' in the famous square in Marrakech. I'm afraid you will have missed him as I personally booked him on the two o'clock sailing from Algeciras in southern Spain to Tangier."

"Yes, I have his itinerary here," added Shay. "From Morocco, he crosses the Sahara and heads for Timbuktu to do an installation called 'Sand in the Gland'. And from there..."

"*Merde!*" cursed the officers as they kicked the wheels of their rickety Citroën deux chevaux police cars. "*Est-il trop tard pour déjeuner?*"

IN SEARCH OF
DAEDALUS

ICARUS SAT SIPPING A frothy cup of café au lait as he stared at his newly purchased KLM ticket from Paris Charles de Gaul to Paramaribo in Suriname, via Amsterdam. It was a Monday afternoon, and the flight wasn't due to leave until Wednesday at seven in the morning, so he was wondering what he should do to fill in the time when a voice spoke to him over his right shoulder.

"You'll need a passport," was all he heard, as he looked up to find the mysterious priest that he had met in the Highland bothy standing over him.

"How and why did...?"

"Because it is my responsibility to look out for you. I made a promise. So, if you intend getting on that flight, you really only have one full day to get a passport; did you not think you'd need one?"

"Who told you that I would be here?" Icarus demanded to know. "I thought you had gone to the Isle of Lewis for some reason or another?"

"That's exactly where I was, I had some business to attend to, and I find it so very beautiful and calming there. I have witnessed many tragic things in my life, and I find that just a few days there walking those dazzling white sands and looking out over the ocean restores me."

"So, answer my question," insisted Icarus, "who told you where I was and what do you want with me?"

"Oh, a little bird told me..."

"Would that little bird be about five-feet-one-inch tall and have a thick Glaswegian accent?"

"Well... err, yes, but don't be cross with her. It was I who influenced Slack-water House to put you into her care. You needed someone unorthodox and strong, and the social services allowed her to take you, in the hope that she would make a mess of things. They were looking for an excuse to get rid of her, because like you, she is a free spirit, an independent thinker, and that was dangerous for them."

"She should have let me know!"

"Look Icarus, she has never met me, and thinks that I am one of the administrators from Slack-water House who needs regular updates on your progress and welfare. Don't be cross with her for she thinks the world of you."

"But I have all kinds of people chasing me, accusing me of being some kind of pervert and wanting to lock me up. Because I display my work, I am accused of being an exhibitionist in a most damning way – perhaps they're right, I don't know, but I don't want to be caught before I at least find my father."

"Please, Icarus, I'd like you to trust me; we should leave the airport and go into the centre of Paris and melt into the crowds. I have a suite at the hotel George Cinque and you are welcome to stay with me. And besides, this airport like all airports these days, is crawling with police, and let's face it you are very easy to spot."

Icarus agreed, not least because he needed help to fast-track his passport application. They went over to the carpark where a car was waiting for them at the far end of the top storey. A middle-aged man dressed as a chauffeur held open the door of a midnight-blue Bentley Mulsanne. *"Gracias Jorge,"* said the priest as he insisted Icarus went first and then joined him in the back seat.

"*Quisiéramos ir a George Cinque, por favor.*"

"*Como vosotros queréis, Padre,*" he replied as he gently closed the car door.

"Jorge has been with me since he was a small boy, but he speaks no English, so anything we discuss will be absolutely confidential."

Icarus was more than a little bit uncomfortable and wondered why should he be discussing anything confidential, and what kind of priest owns such an expensive luxury car and has a chauffeur?

On arrival at the Georges Cinque – probably one of the most luxurious hotels in the world – the staff ran out to greet him as if they were royalty. Jorge helped them with the Louis Vuitton luggage, and they were shown up to their suite by no less than the manager of the hotel. "Very nice to have you staying with us again Padre. I have made all of the usual arrangements."

"Thank you Monsieur Beauprout, I am sure everything will be satisfactory. This is my colleague Mister... err, Smith, he will be staying in the guest room until he departs for the airport early on Wednesday morning, so we'll need a wake-up call about four a.m. if that would be okay."

"*D'accord* Padre, and will there be anything else?"

"Thank you, no, Monsieur Beauprout, that's all for now."

Icarus put his tatty little suitcase down on the bed. He was awestruck. "Jaysus, two of me would fit in this bed!" he gasped. The sheer luxury of his room was unbelievable. Everywhere was decorated with gold-leaf, and fine fabrics tumbled everywhere. The fabulous antique furniture would not have been out of place in the Palace of Versailles and the carpet pile was so deep that it felt as if it came up to his ankles. So, again the question came back to him – what kind of priest commands this kind of wealth?

Icarus kicked off his Doc Martin Boots and slumped onto the bed. He had a silly little conversation with Daisy his dolly, and then got up to run a relaxing bath, but it was a bath the likes of which he had never seen. It had gold fittings and knobs and switches and what looked like drainage holes along the inside. Above it was installed something that resembled a water chute, and to him it looked more like a fairground ride than a bath. He rather warily hit the electric on/off switch, and a soft whirring sound began as all kinds of coloured lights began to flash.

To his amazement a female American voice began to give him instructions: "For a tepid bath at twenty-two-point-five degrees, with no irrigation press button 'A' until an asterisk appears, and then select number one. With irrigation press the same button, wait for the cloud symbol to appear and then select number two, and hold to increase the flow as desired."

"To increase the temperature in gradients of five degrees, depress the on/off switch and hold for five seconds until the high-pitched pips can be heard. For those with hearing difficulties hold for a further five seconds, when the pips will be replaced by a soft vibration. Then turn the dial marked 'D' anti-clockwise when a red light, or vibration, will appear for every five degrees. For comfort and safety, it is not recommended to exceed a temperature of 35 degrees centigrade."

"Holy Jaysus," pleaded Icarus, "I only want a good soak, how do I turn the feckin' taps on?"

The recorded American lady ignored his request and continued: "For recuperative ripple remedy, turn dial 'D' clock-wise and wait for the green lights to appear. When the pump has achieved its optimum pressure, continue to turn clock-wise, then select number three and hold until the desired ripple is reached."

Icarus was becoming impatient. "Look lady, where are the feckin' hot and cold water taps for feck's sake?"

"For accompanying waterfall and/or impulse-jets, lift and turn dial 'C' while holding down the outrider. Failure to hold down the outrider simultaneously will set the programme back to start, and a period of five minutes must be allowed for the system to reboot."

Icarus was going frantic by this time and he angrily pushed and turned every button and dial he could find – but still no water appeared; but what did appear was a loud clunking, followed by a not very healthy sounding bang, and a speeded-up recording that squeaked: "Under no circumstances select any function until the bath is filled to at least a depth of thirty-point-five centimetres.

An instruction manual with further details can be found in the George Cinque folder in the dressing-table drawer."

"What a holy bollix of a twatting carry-on," he cursed. "I think I'll take a shower!"

The shower appeared to be quite normal, so he hung up his George Cinque monogrammed silk dressing gown on the gold coat-hook at the back of the bathroom door and climbed inside. Pressure pads under his feet detected his presence, and soft music emitted from inbuilt speakers as the same female American voice began to speak: "To select either the overhead cascade or the sprinkler head, select button 'A' and turn the..." Icarus immediately jumped out of the shower and scowling he slammed the gold glass shower door behind him. He was not normally a man to let things bother him, but this time he was well and truly wound up. "I'll just have a good sluice down at the sink then," he decided.

All was quite normal at the sink as a movement sensor detected when his hands were under the taps and miraculously, the water flowed, but alas, not constantly; for as soon as he withdrew his hands, the water turned itself off. He looked for a plug so that at least he could fill washbasin, but he could not find one. He had not noticed the knob that needed to be turned clockwise to raise the inbuilt stopper, so he thought he would block up the plughole with toilet paper, but again to his increasing frustration, he couldn't find a single sheet. He searched everywhere, and then sat down on the toilet to get an eyelevel view into what he assumed was the bathroom store cabinet. He then pulled open the doors, but being so tall, he was unable to see inside. It meant that he had to blindly poke about the shelves to feel for a toilet roll – but again there was none to be found. Then suddenly without warning, the Japanese designed high-tech loo, began to make a soft purring sound a bit like a paper-shredder, and then pulsed fine jets of warm water upwards in a wonderfully soporific soothing fashion, followed by puffs of gently perfumed warm drying air. It all cascaded beautifully and Icarus thought it was absolute bliss. He leant back with his hands behind his head and sighed like a Caesar enjoying the decadent luxury of a Roman bath. He then moaned with contentment and declared: "Jaysus, what is it with me and my arse?"

Unable to make any of the washing facilities work for him, he ended up using the toilet to do his ablutions, which made him giggle but it took him an age. By the time he was ready and had knocked on the partition door to the priest's room, there was no answer. The door was not locked, so he pushed it open and entered. In the centre of the room on the Louis Quatorze gold inlaid table, an open street map of Paris had been left for him with a note that simply said, "Enjoy!"

It was eight o'clock in the evening and he thought it would be a great waste to be in romantic Paris and not take full advantage. He picked up his little suitcase to take with him as he did not want any of the domestic staff finding his 'flying man' costume – just in case, and he set off with his heart fluttering in anticipation and excitement for an evening that he was determined he would never forget, or perhaps be unable to remember.

The hotel organised him a taxi and he headed for La Pigalle, and the Moulin Rouge, that he had read so much about and had flown over in his imagination. "I wonder," he laughed to himself, "Is Paris ready for Icarus O'Toole in all his splendour?"

As he paid for his taxi and stepped out onto Boulevard de Clichy, he looked up at the famous Moulin Rouge and was spellbound. This was the theatre that created the famous 'Can-can' dance, and he couldn't wait to see it in all its glory. The pavement outside the box office was heaving and as he waited in line to purchase ticket, a large man in a baseball cap was unceremoniously ejected and bundled out of the front door, where he landed heavily on his backside in front of him.

A muscular bouncer in an immaculate dinner suit and black bow tie stood over him as he smoothed out his sleeves. "We have a strict dress code monsieur. No Bermuda shorts, no trainers, no sweaty vests. Jackets and ties are required at the very least. And neither do we tolerate abuse of the staff."

"My father fought for your country back in nineteen forty-four. There wouldn't have been a Moulin Rouge if not for him and the other American soldiers. It would have either been blown up or renamed the Rote Muhle and used as the Gestapo headquarters!"

The dishevelled American tourist grabbed hold of Icarus by his trouser legs in an attempt to haul himself to his feet. "You won't get in either Mac, not with those scruffy boots. Can you believe they have a dress code in there, where they have semi-naked gals prancing about on stage and hostesses wearing all kinds of bizarre costumes?"

"The name's Wilbur Wisconsin the Third by the way; not from Wisconsin though – from Poughkeepsie, New York, U. S. of A. Pleased to make your acquaintance sir."

"Likewise," smiled Icarus as he held out his hand and introduced himself as John Smith from Achill, County Mayo, I.R.E.L.A.N.D. "So, you don't think I'll get in wearing these boots?"

"No chance, but I wouldn't worry anyway about missing the show, they've only restricted view seats left, I'd come another day if I were you – and book early."

"That's a pity, replied Icarus, I've only one more day here in Paris, and I so much wanted to see the Can-can being danced."

"Well in that case, come with me my friend, I have a couple of tickets for tonight's show at the Folies Bergère, the famous cabaret and music hall theatre on Rue Richer. Mavis, my wife has a headache and can't make it, so I'd appreciate the company."

Icarus had read about the Folies Bergère and was excited at the prospect. He knew that it had been the haunt of great artists, such as Henri Toulouse Lautrec and world-famous performers including Edith Piaf and Marcel Marceau. "Charlie Chaplin once played there, you know," he nodded knowingly.

"Ah yes, and an American broad called Josephine Baker made her name by performing in nothing but a skimpy skirt made from a piece of string around her waist with a few artificial bananas dangling down."

Icarus instantly identified with her but did not want to let on for fear of being discovered. "What brings you to Paris then?" asked Icarus trying to make polite conversation as they walked through the elegant Parisian boulevards towards Rue Richer.

"Oh, business and pleasure, that's why I brought Mavis along to see the most romantic city in the world – pity about her headache, though. Anyway, I'm a talent scout, you know, for the movies and all that crap, and I had a call from an agent friend of mine called Solly Lieberkraut. He insisted I get my ass over to here on the next available flight because he had discovered a sensational new talent over in France. When I got to his hotel, I found that he had frigged off back to the States for some reason without letting me know."

"What a coincidence," said a startled Icarus before he could stop himself, then added, "um, yes... err business and pleasure for me too. Pleasure is my business, I mean, I'm scouting for a bit of pleasure... no I don't mean that... what the feck do I mean?"

"Who gives a fuck, John? John that is your name? Geez I meet so many people..."

Icarus felt guilty for not being truthful, but then added: "It's John... it's easy to remember cos every Tom, Dick and Harry is called John."

Icarus was amazed by how small the world was and felt understandably uneasy. He decided that he should be polite and enjoy the show, but then get out of there as soon as was practicable. The splendid art deco design theatre was packed to the gunnels and the atmosphere was electric, and as soon as the curtains opened, he was in his element. Lines of tall dancers strutted about the stage in ostrich feather head dresses as they revealed themselves then coyly hid behind marvellous feather fans. The full orchestra and jazz-band accompanied a superb quartet of singers, and he had to grip onto his seat tightly for fear of rushing forwards to join them on stage.

The beat of the drums and the plucking of the double base pulsed a seductive rhythm that Icarus felt deep in his body and soul, and his feet began to tap and his bottom bounced up and down his seat in perfect synchronisation. A small ill-tempered lady tapped him on the shoulder complaining that she could not see, but he didn't notice her as he was far too carried away. As his bouncing became more and more excited and exaggerated, she complained to a nearby usherette, who then called over security to sort him out, but by the time a security guard got to his seat, it was vacant.

As though in a trance, Icarus disappeared into the dressing rooms and put on his flying man outfit, grabbed two of the ostrich fans, leapt on stage and joined the line of dancers. Icarus was an amazing if somewhat eccentric dancer and he took centre stage like a colossus. The lighting technician assumed that he was the main act and followed him with the spotlight around the stage, into the aisles, thrice round the audience and over to the rear entrance doors.

The orchestra were in fits of laughter, as were the audience when he paused and held the ostrich fans over himself. They obliged him with a dramatic drumroll, and after it reached a deafening crescendo, he dropped the fans, blew everyone a good-night kiss and ran naked into the Paris night. A massive cheer followed him out of the theatre as he sprinted away. "I was born for this!" he shouted in a state of euphoria as he adjusted his arse feather into a more comfortable position.

Then to his horror, he realised that he had left his little suitcase in the dressing room. The whole of his life was contained in that scruffy eighteen-inch-long suitcase, so it was critical he retrieved it. He quickly turned back and concealed himself by clinging close to the walls like a gecko, and creeping in and out of shadowy doorways.

In his attempt to remain unseen, he disturbed courting couples, down and outs, one ever-so-posh gentleman taking a leak and one not so posh sailor taking a dump. Unsurprisingly they all protested loudly, terrified by the apparition of a six-foot-ten naked man with a large feather stuck up his arse, creeping up on them in the dark.

Much to his dismay, their shouts of alarm drew the attention of two Gendarmes who rushed over to see what the disturbance was. Icarus's clandestine attempt at getting back to the theatre unnoticed was in jeopardy, so he squashed himself flat behind a wooden fence and remained motionless until a nosy Jack Russell terrier discovered him and went berserk.

He bolted into the street and sprinted as fast as his long loping legs would allow, easily outpacing the Gendarmes, but unable to shake off the annoying little dog. He zigzagged at full speed up La Rue Richer, but to no avail as the yapping little pest refused to give up the chase. He only managed to escape when his rudder-feather sprung free and the terrier viciously dived on it and tried to savage it to death.

The Gendarmes were soon on the scene and tried to pick up the feather as evidence, but the snarling Jack Russell refused to let go. It only gave up its prize when one of the Gendarmes tried to separate it from the feather with his foot. It immediately turned its attention to the bottom of his trouser leg and shook it like a newly caught rat. They had absolutely no idea where the fugitive had escaped to, so they turned around with a shrug of their shoulders and set off walking back to the station. "*Zut alors*!" swore one officer as he examined the goose feather whilst dragging and shaking his leg in a vain attempt to cast off the little pest.

Icarus had found a discarded paper tablecloth in a bin behind a restaurant and was wearing it like a cloak so he didn't stand out so much. It had the opposite effect as he ran the last fifty yards to the stage door at the back of the theatre. He looked like a giant Mahatma Gandhi who was just about to miss the very last train to Calcutta as he dived inside and scurried up to the dressing rooms. A public phone had been installed on the landing for the use of the actors, and he could hear Wilbur, the American talent scout pleading on it: "But you gotta get back over here Solly, I've just seen the act of the century – no, the act of the millennium...!"

Icarus closed the dressing room door behind him and to his relief his clothes were still on the peg where he left them with his suitcase sitting underneath. He checked the contents, gave his dolly a little kiss and stuffed his suit and boots into it. Before he closed it, he selected a spare rudder-feather, inserted it with a happy flourish, wrapped the tablecloth around his shoulders and rushed back out into the night. He was determined to perform on top of the Eiffel Tower, as one last grand gesture. "I can't disappoint my public," he announced, "I might never be in Paris again!"

Like a giant white moth, he flew up the Avenue des Champs-Elysées and marvelled at the Arc de Triomphe before crossing over the Seine at the Pont d'Iena to the Eiffel tower. There were plenty of celebrations in Paris that night with plenty of party-goers in fancy dress and he blended in nicely. He took his place in the queue for tickets, and all was going well until it started to rain and his paper tablecloth started to disintegrate. He was saved by a small French lady who gesticulated for him to share her '*parapluie*' but then struggled to cover his head, even when he bent down and she stood on her tippy-toes.

The ticket queue was tightly packed but even so, a few uneasy tourists noticed Icarus's protruding backside complete with feather. Nevertheless, he managed to enter the lift without being challenged, but when he exited at the viewing level, the heavens opened and his tablecloth cloak completely deteriorated. Those tourists looking forward to a spectacular night-time panorama got a view more than was described in the brochure. With the rain pouring and the lightning crashing all around him, Icarus struck up his now infamous flying man's pose and held it as if he had been carved from Carrara marble.

As usual, photographers hoping to make a killing from the tourists were there in numbers, and they snapped away, hoping to sell their photographs to the national newspapers. Icarus buttonholed one and said, "If you want a great picture story, follow me!"

Icarus's blood was up and he was determined to have one last night of madness before he faced up to the *bête noire* that was devouring him. He frantically raced all over Paris, leaping in and out of taxis with the bemused photographer in tow. Nowhere was safe from one of Icarus's creations: he mimicked poses from great works of art such as Michelangelo's David and the ancient Greek carvings of the Dying Slave and the Discus Thrower. He even gave a live performance of Hieronymous Duquesnoy's infamous bronze 'The Mannekin Pis' and disappeared just as the Gendarmes came sauntering in. One amused tourist from England was delighted to be able to tell them that he had just that minute 'pissed off'.

The photographer took action-shots at the Pompidou Centre, the Louvre, the Basilique du Sacré Cœur, the Place de la Bastile, and ended up with a hilarious homage to Victor Hugo's Hunchback on the steps of Notre Dame. All the while a growing and delighted audience chased after them through the streets of Paris, trying to guess where he would appear next. The Gendarmes did the same, but only half-heartedly – the French not being as prudish as many other nations. The fact was that they found it all quite amusing, and maintained a discreet presence, but solely for reasons of safety and crowd control.

The head curator from the Louvre was tipped off by a phone call, and came down to witness what all the fuss was about. It sounded to him like the work of Icarus O'Toole that he had sent one of his assistants to view in Scotland. He had heard great things and was anxious to see his work at first-hand.

The word was that there was to be a big finale at the Père-Lachaise Cemetery, the final resting place of many great luminaries, and by the light of a full moon, hundreds were scrambling over the walls to witness the creation of a new 'Art Nouveau'.

The Gendarmes arrived as did the Mayor of Paris in his official car, but the cemetery did not officially open until eight in the morning and there was a real concern about safety and damage to the graves. The Gendarmes were ordered to keep the crowds back and to allow Icarus to complete his performance to avoid a riot.

Icarus stood with as much dignity as a naked man with a feather up his arse can, by the grave of the revered dancer Isadora Duncan. As he spoke, the photographer interpreted for him: "I stand humbled by the great artists around me: Camille Pissaro; Frederick Chopin; George Bizet; Ireland's own Oscar Wilde; Eugene Delacroix; Sarah Bernhardt; Amedo Modigliani; the list is almost endless. My humble contribution is nothing compared to theirs, I know, but all that I am doing is hoping to inspire a freedom of spirit and thought." Then he gathered himself and took a deep breath before he delivered his iconic statement. With palpable emotion he looked up to the moon and pronounced: "If you don't flap, you can't fly; the sea is blue and so is the sky!"

A polite respectful applause rippled around the cemetery, and Icarus bowed and went behind the gravestone to change back into his corduroy suit. "Show's over," he smiled as he thanked the photographer and shook his hand. He handed him one of Shay Monhue's business cards and asked him if he would send him copies of the pictures, which he was delighted to do.

Icarus also warmly shook hands with everyone, including the Mayor and the curator from the Louvre, however he found it a little strange that his reception in Paris and indeed France had been so welcoming, and he asked them about it.

"We simply love art and artists," replied Monsieur Chantilly, head curator at the Louvre. "We are not a narrow-minded people, we love to love; we invented Champagne – what more can I say?"

Icarus wondered on with a wholesome sense of tranquillity, in and around the cemetery. It was all so peaceful which was a rarity for him, but then he came to a juddering halt. Before him lay the Jewish memorial to the holocaust in remembrance of the thousands of Jews who had been sent to the extermination camps during the Second World War. All around him were disturbing yet powerful sculptures cast in bronze that made him bow his head and fall to his knees. There was one particular sculpture of Auschwitz that consisted of a group of emaciated figures pushing a skeletal corpse in a wheelbarrow. It was so terrible yet so noble in its truth, that it displayed to him a dreadful beauty. It simply made him weep.

"This is what art is for," he said wiping his eyes, "to light the way towards humanity; to banish ignorance and to release us from our baseness by making us look into the darkness that hides in all of our souls."

He stared at it all for a long time, beginning to feel once more like an absolute fraud, and then picked up a small stone and placed it tenderly down on one of the plinths. With that he picked up his scruffy little suitcase and headed off back to his luxurious room at his five-star hotel and muttered sarcastically, "I wonder if Louis Vuitton make a suitcase in this size!"

It was half past three in the morning before Icarus got back to the George Cinque. The night porter greeted him and tried to take his case to carry it up to his room for him, but he declined.

When he entered his room, he tossed his case onto the bed and by force of habit, went to have a shower but quickly did an about turn as he remembered his earlier episode.

He leant over to his side-table to pour himself a glass of water when he found another envelope addressed to Timmy O'Toole. He took a sip of water and then opened it, with his heart beginning to race once more. It read:

> Dear Timmy,
>   Please do not waste your time flying to Suriname on Wednesday: there is nothing to be discovered there. I have it on good authority that Daedalus left some time ago.
>   There is an island in Scotland, off the southwestern coast of the isle of Mull called Iona. It is a place where lost souls often go to find themselves. It is a beautiful place that is also called Holy Island. Perhaps you could find there what your heart most desires – peace.
>   With deepest affection,
>   A well-wisher

Icarus opened the windows and stared out at the Paris skyline. The streets were quiet and the early autumn sun was just beginning to share its morning glow. He was so excited that he ignored his overwhelming desire to sleep and phoned the concierge to organise a taxi to La Gare du Nord in order to catch a train to London, and then on to Edinburgh. He then picked up his suitcase and knocked gently on the priest's door. Again, there was no answer, and as before, he entered the room but this time it had been vacated.

Downstairs at reception, he handed in his keys and asked for his bill. "*Oh non, monsieur Smith,*" said the desk clerk, "it has all been taken care of. *Mais,* one moment please, *attendez!* There is a letter here for you." Icarus took the unmarked envelope and immediately opened it. It contained a brand-new Irish passport for a Timmy O'Toole. "How on earth did he do that so soon?" he asked himself.

As Icarus examined his new passport, a paperboy dumped a load of morning newspapers on the desk. The desk clerk cut the sisal string that bound them together and took a good look at the first page of *Le Monde*. Splashed all over it were dramatic pictures of last night's artistic antics. He peered over his pince-nez spectacles with a knowing smile and remarked: "There is a Eurostar train departing at seven thirteen *précisément* for London monsieur, you have plenty of time. *Au revoir et bon chance.*"

At the train station, Icarus had about half an hour to kill, so he just wandered around and about. The building was elegant and was adorned with stone statues on its façade. He began to toy with the idea of joining them in one final very last pose when he heard his train departure being announced. "Probably for the best," he thought on glancing down at the newspaper stands. His night of artistic triumph had been turned into a night of filth and perversion, by the time the journalists and editors had twisted it all around.

Thinking on his feet, he stuffed his flying man's costume into a carrier bag and gave it to a surprised down and out who was sitting by the front entrance. He then dashed off to security, and went through the inevitable baggage and passport check without incident and took his seat on the train.

At seven thirteen on the dot the train began to pull out of the station. Behind him he could hear the sound of police sirens rushing towards the station. The poor unfortunate beggar had tried on Icarus's costume and was strutting up and down shaking his collection tin with a renewed enthusiasm. Sadly, his moment in the sun was not long lived as officers from Interpol and the Irish Gardaí callously wrestled him to the ground and cuffed him.

Shortly after leaving Paris, a welcome breakfast was served at his seat with plenty of coffee which he was in dire need of. His French trip had drained his reserves more than a little, and he needed a top-up, but the next thing he was aware of was a ticket inspector shaking him by the shoulder, informing him that they had arrived at St Pancras' Station, London. He drowsily pulled himself to his feet and disembarked, then walked slowly along the platform to the barrier. He had to change stations to King's

Cross which was connected to St Pancras' and required just a short walk to catch the two o'clock train to Edinburgh.

As he passed through the barrier a woman in a smart tweed suit was standing with a card held high with the name Mr Timmy O'Toole scrawled on it in black ink marker. "How the feck did anyone...?"

As he approached the woman, she dropped the card from her face to reveal herself. With incredulity Icarus grabbed and hugged her tightly. It was Eva Caber, who had been instructed to meet him there. "The Padre told me to travel with you as far as Edinburgh," she beamed, "and to look out for you."

They were both as pleased as punch as they didn't expect to meet again for a very long time – if ever. It was ideal for Icarus as he hated being alone; he had too much time to stare at his navel, and his over-active imagination often got the better of him and threw him into a panic. They strolled over to King's Cross and waited on the platform for the train, and they passed the time by recounting their recent escapades and then rolling about with laughter.

Before they knew it, the two o'clock train was ready to depart and they climbed on board, Icarus with his little suitcase and Eva with her little knapsack. They both sat facing each other and as the train started up its engines, Eva changed the tone to one regarding serious matters. "Icarus, when you handed me the cheque for forty-million dollars you did it with great indifference. Most people would be running around like demented banshees if that kind of money fell into their laps. I know that you were isolated from the real world for many years when you were in Slack-water House, but do you understand how much forty million dollars is?"

Icarus leant forwards and took hold of both of Eva's hands. "It's a lot of feckin' money Eva, but it is not of much use to me personally. My life can never be as it should have been, and a hundred times that will not change it one iota. I studied and read extensively in my ten years at Slack-water House, and over and over again I learned of the great wrongs done by greedy men. I am certain that if I gave every penny of the forty-million to

Doctor Mead, it still wouldn't be enough; he'd still want more. The trouble isn't the money, for it can be used to do much good. The trouble is man's greed."

"So, have you any idea what you are going to do with it Icarus?"

"Well, I don't intend to give it all away. You know I read somewhere that if you buy a man a fish, you feed him for a day, but if you buy him a net and teach him how to fish, you feed him for a lifetime. So that's the kind of thing I intend to do. For me personally, I neither need nor desire anything."

Eva replied: "Yes I agree with the story of the fish, and it's all very noble... but Icarus, you have and always have had so very little."

"Did you ever study Geoffrey Chaucer at school Eva? Well he relates a story called 'The Pardoner's Tale' that sums up man's nature: Three men drinking in a tavern, gambling and blaspheming, hear the bell signalling the burial of a friend who has been killed, or stolen by death if you like. They vow to go find the one who goes by the name of death and kill him. They are overheard by the Pardoner who informs them that they will find him outside at the foot of an oak tree, and full of bravado they go in search of him."

"By the roots of the oak they find nothing but a bag of gold coins, so they sit down to count their new-found wealth and forget about their appointment with death. Then they decide to spend the night by the tree and leave with their treasure in the morning. They draw lots to see who will go to buy food and wine, and the youngest is chosen, so he set off on his errand. While he is away, he plots to kill the other two by putting rat-poison in the wine, and likewise, his two remaining friends decide to stab him to death on his return. When he arrives with the provisions, they surprise him and murder him; and so pleased are they at their new-found wealth, that they celebrate by drinking the wine and die a slow agonising death."

"So, Eva that is how I see money, and I do try to be optimistic about life, as when I was young on Achill, but I am finding it increasingly difficult. Why even this morning, I saw a poor beggar on the steps of the railway station in Paris. He hated his lot in life, and rightly so, and I watched him implore people to give him just a few meagre cents. I could see in his eyes that he despised those that refused him and despised equally those who gave."

"Only last night in the wee small hours in Paris at the Père-Lachaise cemetery I was reminded of man's terrible capabilities. I stood by the terrifying yet wonderful Jewish Holocaust Memorial. I personally felt a deep shame for the wretchedness of mankind, but did you know there are still people who deny that those terrible things ever happened, even in the face of irrefutable evidence?"

Eva could see that Icarus's wellbeing was taking a nosedive and she did her best to lift him up. "Now cheer up my friend, it's not like you to be so down on yourself. You can't take the whole world on your shoulders." And changing the subject she said, "Tell me, why you are on your way back to Scotland?"

Icarus delved into his jacket pocket and presented her with his latest correspondence from his 'well-wisher'.

"Would you like me to come with you Icarus? Perhaps you should not be on your own on Iona."

Icarus's face lightened up a little, "On my own on Iona? That's catchy!" Then he smiled warmly and replied, "Thank you Eva, I would like that very much."

Icarus soon nodded off again and Eva watched him with concern. Underneath all of the energetic carefree madness, she knew how fragile he really was, and she was concerned that his trip to Iona might not be all that he hoped it would be.

By the time they arrived in Edinburgh, it was early evening, and Eva suggested that they find a nice comfortable B&B and continue their journey in the morning. Even though she could see that Icarus was exhausted, he insisted that that they should not lose any time, and they should find a taxi driver that would take them to the ferry at Oban. "Oh, it's an awful long way Icarus, and by the time we get there, the last sailing to Mull will have departed anyway, and the fare will be awfully expensive."

"I think I could cover that," he said smiling, "and still have a wee bit of change!"

A taxi driver wearing a deep orange turban and a bright smile approached them and spoke to them in a thick Glaswegian accent: "Would ye be needing a taxi madam?"

"Aye," said Eva echoing his tones, "But we need to go to Oban, can you take us that far this evening?"

"Nae problem, hen – but it'll cost ye, but dinnae worry I'll no cheat ye, I'll put it all on the meter. But whoa, is that big bugger with ye? He'll be classed as oversized carriage. He'll be takin' up the whole of the back seat, so it'll be double the fare."

Eva's hackles started to rise, but then recognised the Glaswegian sense of humour and started to smile. "We could tie him on the roof-rack; would that make it cheaper?"

"Aye, it might if I had a roof-rack, so we'll just strap yer pal across the bonnet, nae borra!"

"What the feck' are you two on about?" asked Icarus, unable to fathom their accent.

Eva apologised, "Only messin', when I get with someone from Glasgow, my strong accent comes back. It's a reflex action, but don't worry, he'll take us."

As their luggage was being loaded Eva said that she needed the lavvie, and dashed back into the station where she took the opportunity to make a few important phone calls. When she got back, Icarus was already curled up on the back seat snoring away.

The taxi driver introduced himself as Ravi, and nodded to the back seat and said, "Yer big yin is scannered," and then asked where Eva was from.

"Och I'm a Weegie like you," she replied, "but I've been awa living in Ireland for the past twenty years."

"It's a place I've nivver been," replied Ravi, "I have a wee brother who lives there, and he's always pestering me to visit but I cud nae be arsed. He has a wee eatery called the Taste of India in a toon called Dingle."

Eva was amazed at the coincidence, as was Ravi when she told him that she lived there. "Wid ye ken my brother?" he asked, he was eager to know as much as possible about him and Dingle, which she obliged enthusiastically.

They chit-chatted the whole way to Oban, and the journey seemed to be over in a flash. When Icarus woke, he was stiff as a plank and had trouble prising his long legs out of the taxi. Eva smartly stepped out, took the bags and thanked Ravi for his services.

"Nae problem, I really enjoyed your company. And could I say thank you for no asking me the question that everyone asks me: 'Where are you from?' and when I answer Scotland, they ask again, 'No, where are you really from?' But when I insist that I really am frae Scotland, they mutter not nice things under their breath, or at best tell me that they hope my sore heid will get better soon."

Icarus went to pay for the taxi, but Ravi refused and whispered to him. "The Padre took care of it," then he shook his hand and said, "Bye fer noo – hae a guid journey!"

Icarus again was nonplussed, and he wondered if he was being cared for or manipulated. By the time they had been dropped off it was almost ten o'clock, and as they discussed where they should stay for the night, a large black van pulled up next to them. The driver's window wound down about two inches and a whining little voice followed a flicked-out cigarette butt and enquired, "Would you be looking for accommodation by any chance?"

"I suppose the Padre sent you?" replied Icarus starting to feel a little niffed.

"The who...? Oh no, I drive the van for the Highlander Hotel, I just saw you two standing there with your bags, and I just assumed..."

"Thank you most kindly, sir," interrupted Eva, "your assistance would be most welcome."

Eva and Icarus climbed into the back of the van, and within a few minutes they were registering for a one-night stay, with an early call in the morning for the eight-fifteen ferry to the isle of Mull. After an embarrassing episode where the hotel staff kindly upgraded them to the bridal suite, they each secured a room of their own, met in the dining room for a late supper and went up to bed for a well needed rest.

Icarus slept for about an hour, but then woke up. He struggled with his dark imaginings for the whole night, clinging on to Daisy his dolly for security. He was out of his mind with worry for what tomorrow would bring and managed to fall asleep just as a knock on the door woke him for his six-thirty call and pot of tea.

After a sluggish start, Eva and Icarus met for breakfast in the dining room. Eva ordered the full works including porridge, and Icarus who couldn't face food ordered a couple of sausages just to keep Eva happy.

"Are you going to eat those Icarus, or just chase them around with your fork?" chided Eva, sensing that he was troubled.

"Oh no Eva, I'm just going to frighten them for a while and then stab them in the arse," and then as usual they both started to laugh.

"Don't worry about today Icarus, everything will be fine – you'll see."

"How could you possibly know Eva? Some enigmatic priest whom you all seem to know and refer to him as the Padre – a man with far too much wealth than he should have – is the key to all of this nonsense? I don't even know who or what I am expecting to find on Iona... Jaysus, I just don't know."

They finished their breakfast in silence and then went to their rooms to gather their belongings and met at the reception desk to pay their bill.

"Oh, Mr O'Toole, the bill was settled late last night after you had gone to bed," said the receptionist as she fumbled about under the desk. "There is also a letter here for you that was left at the same time," and with that she handed over the exact same kind of envelope as used by the well-wisher. Icarus tore it open with impatient hands and read its contents.

"What does it say?" asked Eva dying to know.

"Just two words Eva: seek Macbeth."

"What the feck does that mean?"

"I'll be fecked if I know!" puffed Icarus.

Eva in her no nonsense yet cheery manner, told Icarus that it was possible to hire bikes on Mull and suggested that it would be a nice thing to do, to cycle over to the ferry on the west of the island rather than go by taxi.

"It would clear our heads, and we could make little stops along the way and talk things through. You know things never seem so bad in the clear light of the day and the beautiful fresh air. There are plenty of ferries, so time is not a problem – we needn't rush."

"Oh, I don't know Eva; bikes and I don't seem to mix well. Jaysus, my arse feather kept slipping out like a stick in a paste bucket after last time!"

At the ferry terminal in Craignure, they both mounted their bikes and set off on their twenty-four miles or so jaunt across to the ferry at Fionnphort. "Feck me Eva, you could convince a concert pianist that it would be easier to perform wearing boxing gloves!"

For most of the way they rode side by side through wild and desolate country, talking about all kinds of silly things until they decided to have a little break and refreshments in the small village of Bunessan. Being very aware that they were close to Iona they remained silent over their tea and scones, until Icarus chirped up: "Did you remember to bring the calamine lotion Eva?"

After another five miles they arrived at Fionnphort and stood with their mouths open. The coastline was a marvellous mixture of white sandy beaches and pink granite rocks washed by a pure turquoise and jade sea. Iona shone out of it clothed in emerald green and was a truly uplifting sight.

"There can be nothing to fear Icarus," remarked Eva, "in such a beautiful place."

"Yes," agreed Icarus as he gazed open-mouthed across the shining sea, "beauty WILL save the world."

The ferry journey was only a few minutes and before they knew it, they were standing on the sacred isle.

"Can you feel it Icarus? It's like a warm hug from heaven. It's all around us, under our feet and in the air – it's perfect."

Icarus completely ignored her and asked an old man who was disembarking if Macbeth had any connection with Iona.

"Aye young man, he's with the forty-eight other Scottish kings resting in the burial ground by St Oran's chapel behind the abbey just over there."

Icarus thanked him and apologised to Eva. "I'm sorry Eva, I cannot share in your beliefs of heaven and hell and all of that rubbish."

Eva was more than a little taken aback as she always considered Icarus to be a spiritual person, but she decided not to pursue the matter knowing his delicate state of mind, but unprompted he continued as they walked towards the abbey.

"The happy-clappies regularly came to Slack-water House to try to save our souls and bring us the teachings of the Bible. I was encouraged to pray for forgiveness for my sins, for that was the only way into the kingdom of heaven. They told me that my sins had brought me to where I was, and that I would never find salvation unless I was truly repentant."

"Eva, my love for Daisy Maisie was the most beautiful and natural thing in the world. Far more beautiful even than all of this majestic scenery around us, and how could it ever have been something that was filthy and displeased God?"

"I screamed at them to feck off and not be bothering my head, and mercifully they left me alone after that. So, you see Eva, knowing what I do about the terrible deeds of the pious nuns at St Vergüenza's, and my doubts about a Padre with far too much cash when so much of the world is starving, I think we'll give the subject of religion a wide berth!"

Eva nodded and left Icarus to himself, and went into the abbey trying to imagine St Columba who founded it, and the monks that created the beautiful Book of Kells. She had marvelled at the stunning Bible displayed in Trinity College Dublin, and had promised herself one day, to visit the place that had inspired its creation.

Outside in the burial ground Icarus said to himself, "Well this is where you would seek Macbeth, but there's not much here to see."

Then a small hand of a young boy slipped into his, which in turn held the hand of a woman dressed in a hooded cloak. They both stood in front of him and she slowly dropped her hood to reveal herself. The young boy turned to her and asked: "Is this my daddy?" and she lovingly answered, "Yes, it is my son."

On Beautiful Iona

EPILOGUE

O_N THE FATEFUL DAY of Daisy Maisie's disappearance, Icarus's father, Tomás Gogarty, had been passing underneath the cliffs at Croaghaun in his small fishing boat that he often used for his smuggling runs. The powerful Atlantic westerlies were blowing furiously, creating a powerful updraft as she despairingly stepped out over the cliffs. Miraculously, the wind filled her skirt like a parachute and her fall of seven hundred feet became a gentle glide to the ocean below, where at huge risk to himself, he heroically managed to drag her from the thunderous waves.

She was almost drowned and freezing cold, so he rushed her to his secret booty store and covered her with blankets and cared for her. She faded in and out of consciousness for days, refusing to take any warm drink or food that he offered to her. It became obvious to him that she had lost the will to live and that she required a different kind of warmth. Over the following month, he was very tender and kind to her, and eventually, after her cruel treatment from the nuns, she responded and began to take a little food, and gain a little strength.

He needed to get out of the country fast, and his caring for Daisy Maisie had delayed him and put him in jeopardy. Not really caring anything for herself or where she ended up, she didn't mind pretending that she was his daughter to aid his escape. In the dead of night, they managed to steal away and head for the port of Cobh in Cork where they boarded a merchant vessel to Sydney, Australia.

Daisy Maisie grew little by little in strength, but she suffered from seasickness for the whole journey. When they arrived, the ship's doctor told him that his daughter was pregnant, and that had been the cause of her vomiting, and because she was still weak, she would need very special care.

From what she had told him, he guessed that he would be the child's grandfather, and that was the one thing that changed his life for the better. He grew to love her as his true daughter, and when the child was born, he swore that he would never again be the selfish man that so cruelly abandoned his wife and son.

He became a very wealthy man and eventually they went to live in South America where he married a kind and beautiful woman called Dolores de la Hidalgo. They both loved Daisy Maisie and as it turned out to be, their grandson, but she remained emotionally very fragile and flew into a panic at the idea of ever returning to Ireland. She never spoke of Icarus as his memory was deeply painful to her, but after years of a loving environment she slowly began to heal.

After his wife died, Icarus's father was inconsolable and he vowed to put right all of the wrongs that he had been responsible for. As he was still regarded as a felon, he disguised himself as a priest and made the occasional trip to Ireland to see how he could help his son. He was distraught at Icarus's condition and resigned himself to the fact that Slack-water House was probably the best place for him.

He took Daisy Maisie to an orthodontist in New York who did an incredible repair on the damage done to her by the nuns at St Vergüenza's, and with a renewed film-star smile, her confidence grew and she was able to talk about Icarus once more.

When he fell ill with the same tropical illness that his wife died of, everything took on a sense of urgency. The enigmatic Padre was in fact Tomás (Daedalus) Gogarty and not even Eva guessed his true identity, right to the very end. He had embroidered the truth when he met Icarus, not just for fear of rejection, but to make sure that he was ready and able to meet the one true love of his life – Daisy Maisie. He also wanted to make sure that he would be capable of spending his inheritance wisely: Icarus passed on all counts.

The very morning of Icarus's arrival on Iona, just minutes before he stepped off the ferry, he sadly lost his struggle to live. He had been hanging on with the last vestiges of his strength to greet his long-lost son openly, and to beg for his forgiveness – but it was not to be. When Icarus learned the truth of his father, he was devastated, but he was comforted by Daisy Maisie and his son whom she had named Tomás after his grandfather.

Over the following years, he spent his fortune wisely, and with the help of a few philanthropic donations here and there, he was able to repair his somewhat eccentric reputation. As he could afford the best lawyers, Doctor Mead was convicted of fraud and corruption, and was sentenced to seven years in Mountsad prison, as were four of his closest allies. He was publicly denounced and his victims compensated, or as Icarus put it: "We gave that sleeveen a good pruning."*

He purchased Renmort Pitch and Putt golf course, redesigned it and reopened it as the biggest crazy-golf course in the world. Every year they held a huge pro-celebrity charity event raising funds for mental health. The celebrity in each team of four, was an inmate at Slack-water House and it always proved to be a great success. Everyone wanted to have Mr McTweezer in their team, as his excuses and outbursts after fluffing a shot were hilarious. They were fantastical works of pure poetry, and Shay Monhue approached him about producing a literary compilation. Mr McTweezer told him to go poke a rhinoceros up the arse, and then he agreed with a grin.

He bought St Vergüenza's from Sister Rencoroso, who by then was a gibbering inmate at Slack-water House, and turned it into a concert and dance hall in an attempt to exorcise the ghosts of brutality that had haunted its cold corridors. When his lawyer pointed out the questionable legality of her signing a contract in

---

* Irish slang: being squeezed hard by the testicles as a few garsúns hold you down.

190

her mental state, he asked if anyone had questioned her mental state when she was inflicting acts of barbarity on young vulnerable girls under her care.

Daisy Maisie even went to visit her and forgave her, but Icarus was never able to do so. A very old nun approached her when she was there and took her hands and kissed them. She told her that she had worked in the office at St Vergüenza's and had not witnessed any of the awful goings on there. When she heard about her and Icarus's terrible fate, she felt deeply ashamed and became the Good Samaritan that brought him bits and pieces to his little cottage, before he was taken away to Slack-water House. It had remained her secret for all of her life.

One fine afternoon in early June, Icarus's little family visited the cliffs of Croaghaun. He was very worried for Daisy Maisie as the memory of her traumatic fall could have been too much for her, but he needn't have worried – she was fine. The joy of being together at last, and memories of happier times past, proved to be a great healer. As they strolled across the tops, they broke into a jog, then ran and spun and danced until dizzy. In the intoxicatingly fresh air, they all tumbled and fell into the sweet-smelling long grass, laughing and giggling as in the happy crazy days when Icarus and Daisy Maisie were carefree children together.

As Icarus and his son enthusiastically discussed all kinds of serious nonsense, Daisy Maisie hung a daisy chain about both of their necks and kissed them tenderly. "The chains are my gift of love to you both, but they must be handled gently and treasured because they are so easily broken, as are our hearts."

Icarus put his hand into his inside pocket and pulled out an envelope which he gave to her. "Since this found its way back to me it has remained next to my heart."

Daisy Maisie opened it and revealed the daisy chain that she had given him all those years ago. Her eyes filled with tears of joy as she showed her son that the flowers had not faded in the slightest, and the chain that had remained unbroken for all of those years.

The following spring, Icarus and Daisy Maisie had the most wonderful wedding party. Eva Caber was Icarus's best man

– naturally; and for the craic, Donald Macleod and Angus McBreen were the bridesmaids. Père Paul conducted a rather unconventional service, as members of the Gay Rights Brigade stood guard of honour in the middle of the beach at Keem Strand at the foot of mighty Croaghaun. Major Ince and his wife Jenny together with a full battalion of commandos turned up in full military attire, with all the regalia including flags and banners. Their regimental mascot, a pretty blond nanny goat, proudly paraded in front of them, dressed up in a decorated tabard emblazoned with the commandos' colours, but it somehow managed to slip its lead, and raced away before anyone could catch it.

They were joined by countless guests, both invited and uninvited, from Roscoff and other parts of France. No one wanted to miss one of Icarus's legendary celebrations. The Mayor of Paris also attended, as did the chorus line and musicians from the Folies Bergère. Holly and Molly Macleod piped in their version of 'The Wedding March' and were then joined by the full forty members of the neighbouring Clew Bay Pipe Band. The music was thunderous and emotional and could be heard as far away as Westport, some thirty miles away.

Mr McTweezer turned up with Doctor de Grave, who struggled to stop him from making a speech. He had been working on it for weeks, but when Doctor de Grave saw his notes, he was horrified. Fearing a tirade of obscenities, he hoped to curtail his oration by persuading him to propose the toast to the bride and groom. Mr McTweezer thought it was a splendid idea, and didn't seem to notice when after his opening line, the Clew Bay Pipe band, together with all of the other musicians, completely drowned out his creative language.

The official wedding photograph was taken of course by Pappa Ratzi, who also recorded it on video. He thought it would make a great entry for the short-film category at the Cannes Film Festival, which is what he did the very next year. It was rejected however, mainly because Mr McTweezer had been asked by Pappa to do the voice-over: "For to make for it a surreal artistic atmosfera." Being unable to understand hardly a word Mr McTweezer

Celebrations at Keem Strand

spoke, an unfathomable and utterly obscene soundtrack had condemned his film to the cutting-room floor.

For a man who had felt terribly alone for so much of his life, Icarus O'Toole had thousands of people cheering and wishing him and his new bride every happiness. It was all recorded and immortalised by the admiring pen of Shay Monhue who rejuvenated his career as an author and published a best seller entitled 'Slapstick Solutions for Serious Situations'. It was sold in one hundred and ninety-four countries.

High on the summit of Croaghaun, a magnificent boc goat stood like a sentinel and stared down at the gathering below. As he nonchalantly chewed a mouthful of delicious daisies, he proceeded to shag hell out of the commando's mascot nanny. A terrified old man spotted it, but being unable to call out in fear, he just pointed at it open mouthed with his walking stick in his trembling hand. In an attempt to flee the beast, he tried to spin his wheelchair round, but only managed to tip himself sideways into the sand. When everyone rushed to help him, they all looked up to the summit of Croaghaun, but there was nothing to be seen, apart from the mist as it rolled gently down the mountainside.

Icarus O'Toole, The Incredible Naked Flying Man of Achill, continued on his artistic journey, and a fabulous artbook was eventually produced as promised. It also proved to be a best-seller and had rave reviews in the art world and beyond. Shortly afterwards he was awarded two special honours from the President of France for services to art and culture. Gold medallions had been specially struck by the École des Beaux-Arts and the Académie Française, and presented to him at a special dinner in Paris.

The administrators from the Arts Council tried to creep and crawl up to him, and he had a lot of fun making them squirm. He completed an even more disrespectful Arts Council grant application, and sent the form in to them for their consideration. It was accepted eagerly and immediately. It was a request for funding for his proposed crucifixion, to be staged on the top of Croagh Patrick on Reek Sunday.* His lovely new wife Daisy

* Annual day of pilgrimage up Ireland's holy mountain.

Maisie O'Toole tried hard to persuade him that it would be a step too far, and he just winked at her.

"Of course it would be darling; but think of the bother those Arts Council buffoons will have, trying to justify their blasphemous decision when the Church and all of Ireland finds out!"

Ireland's Holy Mountain

Icarus O'Toole's Thesaurus

"If there is wind, let it flow, especially if it's down below."

"The sky's not the limit – that's where it begins."

"Laugh and the world laughs with you, cry and you fly alone."

"Trying to be good is a devil of a job."

"One good turd deserves another."

"An open mind flies like a bird, but a closed mind sinks like a turd."

"It ain't over 'til the fat lady farts."

"Don't bite off more than you can poo."

"A faint fart never won a fair lady."

"Great minds stink alike."

"It would be easier for a rich man to piss through the eye of a needle, than to enter the kingdom of heaven."

"Eat drink and be merry for tomorrow we'll fly."

"If you think lunatics are crazy, you should hear what they think about you."

"It's called a willy 'cos it's designed to be silly."

"A guilty conscience is the toilet paper of mankind."

"A perfumed rose has its roots in horseshit."

"Dancing is flying for the earthbound."

"Great art reveals the soul, but in my case – my artsoul."

"What is it with me and my arse?"

＊ Thesaurus: Greek, a storehouse. Pronounced by Icarus as 'the sore arse'.

Icarus' Further Works

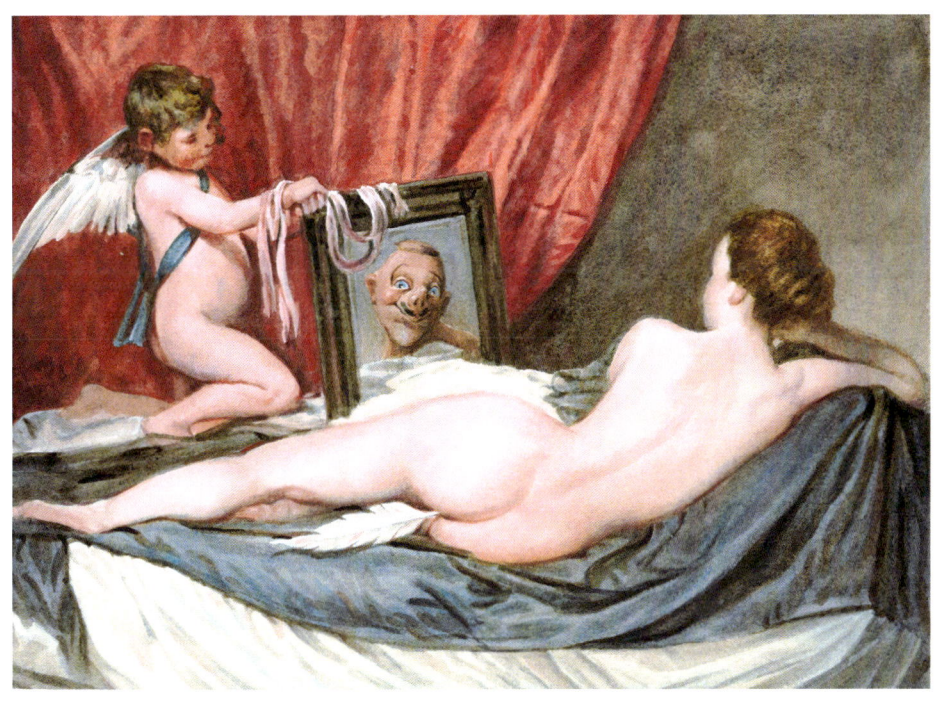

THE END